BAR BITES

A Man of the Month Cookbook

Brenda – Great meeting you at RORZ2019! xxoo J.K

Bar BITES

A MAN OF THE MONTH COOKBOOK

SHORT STORIES & SLICES OF LIFE BY
NEW YORK TIMES BESTSELLING AUTHOR

J. KENNER

RECIPES FROM *USA TODAY* BESTSELLING AUTHOR

SUZANNE M. JOHNSON

EVIL EYE
CONCEPTS

Bar Bites: A Man of the Month Cookbook

Copyright 2018

J. Kenner

Recipes

Copyright 2018

Suzanne McCollum Johnson

ISBN: 978-1-948050-09-8

Published by Evil Eye Concepts, Incorporated

Table of Contents

OCTOBER

NOVEMBER

DECEMBER

Introduction

When I first envisioned the *Man of the Month* series, the initial spark of inspiration centered on friendship. Specifically, a group of friends who band together to try to save The Fix on Sixth, their favorite bar, by putting on a Man of the Month calendar contest.

As I got into plotting the series, though, the friendship aspect really came to the forefront. It wasn't just about the bar, it was about each other. Friends falling in love. Friends helping each other through tough times. Friends joking and teasing. And the circle of friends continually expanding as new characters came into the mix.

And, of course, there was eating and drinking. Which led to this cookbook. (Because, hey, *friends, eating, drinking*. It's the perfect trifecta, right? And it only gets better when you throw books into the mix!)

But all of that brings me full-circle back to the concept of friends. This time not fictional ones, but real ones. Because it's my real life friends, starting with the amazing Liz Berry, who truly made this cookbook happen.

I met Liz years ago, and after *Release Me* came out, she asked me to be part of Evil Eye's 1001 Dark Nights publishing program. Since she's awesome and the idea behind 1001 is brilliant (created by Liz and MJ Rose together), I eagerly said yes.

From there, much like in the stories, the friendship expanded. Through Liz, I met cool folks like her husband, Steve Berry (excuse me while I have a fan girl moment), and her sister, Suzanne M. Johnson (who co-authors this cookbook and is *amazing*), and a slew of authors who've became friends. In some cases, I became reacquainted with authors I'd known for years, but had previously known mostly as an acquaintance. Liz has a gift for bringing people together and acting as a midwife (she'll probably hate that word–too bad!) for an author's creation of stories!

One of the authors I already knew, but got to know better, was the inimitable Lexi Blake, one of my absolute favorite people. Since meeting again through Liz, we've hung out together on vacations and retreats, worked together on projects such as Rising Storm and the Lexi Blake Crossover Collection (my story is *Justify Me*). And with this cookbook, I'm doing her the dubious honor of basically saying, "That's awesome! I want to be you and do it, too!"

You see, a few years ago, a group of authors were hanging out at Liz's place in Florida, and she introduced us to her sister, Suzanne. Now, Suzanne is as warm and wonderful as she can be, full of Southern hospitality and all that good stuff. So I would have adored her no matter what. But folks, that woman can *cook*. Like seriously. Like I gained a pant size on that trip. A-Maz-Ing.

It turns out that Lexi had known Suzanne for a while, and they had been working with Liz on *Master Bits & Mercenary Bites* (it's great; go one-click. I'll wait).

During that trip, Suzanne used us as guinea pigs for some of those recipes. Did I mention the pant size? Yeah, it was all *that good.*

Fast forward to me planning the Man of the Month series. I have a calendar that goes along with the series (twelve books, twelve hot guys!) and because the owner of the The Fix, Tyree, is also a chef, I thought a cookbook would be fun. And since I thought that *Master Bits & Mercenary Bites* was the best thing ever, I made a phone call…

Thankfully, both Liz and Suzanne thought the idea sounded fabulous! And the result is this cookbook, with slices of life from characters in the series, and a whole new short story featuring two characters who've been lusting after each other, but never got a book! Now they do!

So huge hugs to Liz and Suzanne and Lexi… and all the friends in that circle. And also to all the readers of the series who've gotten drawn into the world of The Fix on Sixth. Thanks for making the characters your friends!

XXOO

J. Kenner

january

MASHED MARTINIS
LOBSTER ROLLS
LEMON ICEBOX PIE SHOTS
> DIRTY MARTINI WITH BLUE CHEESE STUFFED OLIVES

february

MUSHROOM SPINACH RISOTTO BALLS
VEGGIE PUFF PIZZA
LASAGNA ROLLS
> AMERICANO WITH CANDIED ORANGE SLICES

march

SKILLET BUFFALO DIP WITH HOMEMADE TORTILLAS
VEGGIEDILLAS WITH AVOCADO DIPPING SAUCE
HONEY SRIRACHA CHICKEN TACOS
> BLOODY MARY WITH CANDIED BACON

slice of life
All I Need:
Reece & Jenna

Mashed Martinis

Martinis and mashed potatoes, you ask? Why yes! What better way to jazz up a boring potato than to serve it in a martini glass. The delicious toppings make this a stunning side for a great steak or a showpiece appetizer for any occasion.

MASHED POTATOES

8 large baking potatoes, peeled and quartered

8 tablespoons (1 stick) butter, melted

½ cup milk

1 tablespoon mayonnaise

1 tablespoon salt

1 teaspoon pepper

In a large pot of boiling water, add the potatoes and boil for 15-20 minutes or until tender. Drain potatoes and place in a large bowl. Add the butter, milk, mayonnaise, salt and pepper. Mash with a potato masher or fork. Scoop potatoes into your favorite martini glass and top with desired topping below.

GARLIC PARMESAN SHRIMP

4 tablespoons butter

1 pound jumbo (16-20 count) shrimp, peeled and deveined

2 cloves minced garlic

1 tablespoon flour

1 cup chicken broth

½ cup grated Parmesan cheese

In a large saucepan over low heat, melt the butter and add the shrimp and garlic. Sauté for 3 minutes or until the shrimp are pink, but not completely cooked through. Sprinkle the shrimp with the flour and stir to make a roux. Slowly add the chicken broth, stirring constantly until thickened. This will take about 2-3 minutes. Remove from heat. To serve, place shrimp over mashed potatoes and sprinkle with Parmesan cheese.

FILET AND BLUE CHEESE

4 (4-6 ounce) filet mignon steaks

2 tablespoons Montreal steak seasoning

4 tablespoons butter

2 tablespoons olive oil

1 tablespoon flour

1 cup heavy cream

1 teaspoon salt

1 teaspoon pepper

¼ cup crumbled blue cheese

Preheat oven to 250 degrees. Rub steaks with steak seasoning. In a medium iron skillet over medium high heat, melt 2 tablespoons butter and 1 tablespoon oil. Sear steaks on each side for 2 minutes. Place steaks in the oven for 8-10 minutes or until a meat thermometer reaches 145 degrees for medium rare. Remove steaks from the oven and place on a cutting board. Tent with foil and allow steak to rest for 10 minutes. Place iron skillet over low heat with steak drippings and melt remaining butter and oil. Add flour and stir to make a roux. Slowly add heavy cream, salt and pepper. Stir until thickened. Add blue cheese and stir until combined. Thinly slice filets and place over mashed potatoes. Top with blue cheese sauce.

BACON AND CHEDDAR

1 pound bacon

2 tablespoons flour

1 cup milk

2 cups shredded sharp cheddar cheese

Slice bacon into 1 inch pieces. In a medium skillet over medium heat, cook bacon pieces until crispy. Drain on paper towels. Drain all but 1 tablespoon of bacon grease. Return skillet to low heat and add flour. Stir until a roux forms. Slowly add milk and stir until thickened. Add cheddar cheese and stir until combined. Top mashed potatoes with cheddar sauce and sprinkle with crumbled bacon.

Lobster Rolls

9 lobster tails, cooked and cut into 1 inch pieces

1 cup chopped celery

½ cup mayonnaise

Juice of 1 lemon

¼ cup chopped parsley

½ teaspoon Cajun seasoning

8 hotdog buns

8 tablespoons (1 stick) butter, melted

In a large bowl, combine the lobster, celery, mayonnaise, lemon juice, parsley and Cajun seasoning. Brush each hotdog bun on the inside with melted butter, fill with lobster and serve.

Lemon Icebox Pie Shots

1 (6 ounce) can frozen lemonade concentrate, thawed

2 (8 ounce) containers frozen whipped topping, thawed

1 (14 ounce) can sweetened condensed milk

1 box Nilla wafers

24 shot glasses

In a large bowl, using a hand mixer, combine lemonade concentrate, 1 container whipped topping and sweetened condensed milk. Place wafers in a large resealable bag and crumble, using a rolling pin. To build pie shots, place 1 tablespoon of crumbled wafers on the bottom of each shot glass, then add 1 tablespoon lemon filling, followed by 1 tablespoon of whipped topping. Sprinkle with crumbled wafers.

Dirty Martini with Blue Cheese Stuffed Olives

2 ounces Grey Goose vodka

½ ounce dry vermouth

½ ounce olive juice

2 queen green olives, unstuffed

1 tablespoon blue cheese

Mix vodka, vermouth and olive juice in a cocktail mixer with 3-4 ice cubes. Pour into a martini glass. Stuff olives with blue cheese and place on a toothpick. Serve with martini.

Mushroom Spinach Risotto Balls

2 tablespoons butter

2 cups sliced mushrooms

½ cup diced Vidalia onion

2 cups Arborio rice

½ cup white wine

7 cups chicken broth

1 cup grated Parmesan cheese

Salt and pepper to taste

1 box of frozen spinach, thawed and drained

2 cups all-purpose flour

4 eggs

4 cups panko breadcrumbs

6 cups oil, for frying

MUSHROOM RISOTTO

In a medium saucepan over medium heat, melt one tablespoon of butter and add the mushrooms. Cook until soft, about 5 minutes. Remove the mushrooms and set aside. Add the other tablespoon of butter to the same saucepan over low heat and add the onion. Cook until tender, about 3 minutes. Add rice, stirring constantly for 2 minutes, then pour in wine and stir for an additional 2 minutes. Add 1 cup of chicken broth to the rice and stir until absorbed. Continue this process until all the broth has been added and the rice is tender, approximately 25-30 minutes. Never quit stirring. That's the most important part. Remove from heat and stir in the mushrooms and ½ cup of Parmesan. Add salt and pepper to taste. Spread risotto on a large cookie sheet, cover and refrigerate overnight.

TO MAKE BALLS:

Combine mushroom risotto, ½ cup Parmesan and spinach in a large bowl. Roll into 1 inch balls and coat with flour. Place on a cookie sheet and refrigerate for 30 minutes. Heat oil in a Dutch oven or deep fryer to 350 degrees. In a medium bowl, whisk the eggs. In a separate medium bowl, add the panko breadcrumbs. Remove the balls from the refrigerator and dredge each one in the egg then panko breadcrumbs. Place 4 balls at a time in the oil and fry 1-2 minutes or until golden brown. Drain on paper towels.

Veggie Puff Pizza

1 package (2 sheets) puff pastry

2 tablespoons butter

1 tablespoon oil

1 cup sliced onion

1 cup sliced baby bella mushrooms

1 cup sliced bell pepper (red, yellow or green)

1 cup basil pesto

4 Roma tomatoes, sliced

2 cups shredded mozzarella cheese

Preheat oven to 400 degrees. Unfold each pastry sheet onto a lightly floured surface. Roll sheets out into a rectangle and place on separate greased baking sheets. Bake for 8-10 minutes or until pastry is golden brown. While the pastry is baking, heat butter and oil over medium heat in a medium skillet. Add onion, mushrooms, and bell peppers and sauté until tender, about 8-10 minutes. Spread ½ cup basil pesto over each pastry sheet and top with tomatoes, sautéed veggies and mozzarella cheese. Bake for 5 more minutes or until cheese is melted. Slice and serve.

Lasagna Rolls

1 pound ground beef, cooked and drained

1 (45 ounce) jar of your favorite marinara sauce

12 lasagna noodles

1 (32 ounce) container ricotta cheese

¼ cup basil pesto

1 egg

½ cup grated Parmesan

2 cups shredded mozzarella cheese

Preheat oven to 350 degrees. Combine beef and marinara sauce. Cook noodles according to package. Drain and place noodles flat on parchment paper. Combine ricotta cheese, basil pesto, egg and Parmesan cheese in a medium bowl and spread evenly on noodles. Place half of the marinara sauce in a 9x13-inch baking dish. Roll noodles with cheese mixture from end to end and place on top of sauce. Spread remaining meat sauce over rolled noodles and top with mozzarella cheese. Bake for 20 minutes.

Americano with Candied Orange Slices

2 ounces Campari

2 ounces sweet vermouth

2 ounces club soda

Candied orange slice

Pour first three ingredients into a cocktail shaker filled with 3-4 ice cubes. Shake well and pour into a cocktail glass. Garnish with Candied Orange Slice.

CANDIED ORANGE SLICES

1 navel orange

1 cup water

¾ cup granulated sugar

Thinly slice orange, discarding the ends. In a medium saucepan, bring water and sugar to a boil, stirring to combine. Add orange slices and reduce heat to low. Simmer for 15-20 minutes. Remove slices and place on wax paper. Cool completely before adding to Americano.

Skillet Buffalo Dip with Homemade Tortillas

2 (8 ounce) packages cream cheese, softened

1 (16 ounce) bottle blue cheese dressing

1 (16 ounce) bottle buffalo wing sauce (½ bottle for a milder taste)

3 cups cooked chicken, shredded

1 cup shredded sharp cheddar cheese

Combine the first 3 ingredients with a hand mixer. Add shredded chicken and cheddar cheese and stir until blended. Pour mixture into 4 (3 inch) iron skillets or ramekins. Cook for 10-15 minutes or until bubbly. Serve with Homemade Tortillas.

HOMEMADE TORTILLAS

8 (6-inch) flour tortillas

2 tablespoons oil

1 teaspoon ranch seasoning

Preheat oven to 350 degrees. Cut each tortilla into six triangles. In a medium bowl, toss tortillas, oil, and ranch seasoning until coated. Place chips on a cookie sheet and bake for 10 minutes or until golden brown. Serve with Skillet Buffalo Dip.

Veggiedillas with Avocado Dipping Sauce

4 tablespoons butter

1 cup sliced onion

1 cup sliced baby bella mushrooms

1 cup sliced bell pepper (red, yellow or green)

1 packet taco seasoning mix

¼ cup water

8 burrito size flour tortillas

Nonstick cooking spray

2 cups shredded Mexican cheese blend

In a medium skillet over low heat, melt butter and sauté onions, mushrooms, and bell pepper for 8-10 minutes. Add taco seasoning and water. Simmer for 5 more minutes and remove from heat. In a medium skillet over low heat, coat with cooking spray and lay a tortilla flat in the skillet. Cover half of the tortilla with sautéed veggies and cheese. Then fold the empty side on top of the mixture and allow to cook for 2 minutes, pressing down with a spatula. Next, flip the quesadilla and cook for an additional 2 minutes. Remove from heat and repeat this process with remaining ingredients. Cut quesadillas into thirds and serve with Avocado Dipping Sauce.

AVOCADO DIPPING SAUCE

2 avocados

½ cup plain Greek yogurt

1 teaspoon minced garlic

½ teaspoon salt

Juice of 1 lime

In a stand-up mixer, add avocado, yogurt, garlic, salt, and lime. Blend on low for 1 minute. Serve with Veggiedillas.

Honey Sriracha Chicken Tacos

Oil for frying

6-8 boneless, skinless chicken breast tenders

3 cups flour

1 tablespoon seasoning salt

3 eggs

½ cup milk

8 (6-inch) flour tortillas

Heat oil in a deep fryer or Dutch oven to 350 degrees. Cut the chicken tenders into 1-inch chunks. Mix together the flour and seasoning salt. In a separate medium bowl, whisk together the eggs and milk. Place the chicken in the egg mixture. Take 6 chicken pieces at a time and dredge in flour, shaking off excess. Fry chicken in the oil until golden brown, about 4-6 minutes. Remove from oil and drain on paper towels. Continue with remaining chicken.

SLAW

½ cup mayonnaise

1 tablespoon sugar

2 tablespoons white vinegar

1 (16 ounce) bag of tri-color slaw

Mix together mayonnaise, sugar and vinegar until sugar is dissolved. Pour over slaw and mix well. Refrigerate for at least 2 hours before serving.

HONEY SRIRACHA SAUCE

1 cup of honey

¼ cup of mayonnaise

¼ cup of Sriracha

Add all ingredients to a small blender and mix on low for about 1 minute.

TO SERVE:

On each flour tortilla, place 3-4 chicken tenders, top with 2 tablespoons of slaw, and drizzle with 2 tablespoons of Honey Sriracha Sauce. Fold tortillas in half.

Bloody Mary with Candied Bacon

2 ounces Grey Goose Vodka
4 ounces tomato juice
½ teaspoon hot sauce
1 teaspoon horseradish
1 teaspoon Worcestershire sauce
¼ teaspoon celery seed
¼ teaspoon salt
¼ teaspoon pepper

Fill pint glass with ice. In a separate glass, stir all ingredients together until blended. Pour over ice and garnish with Candied Bacon.

CANDIED BACON

½ cup dark brown sugar
½ cup honey
½ teaspoon cayenne pepper
12 slices bacon

Preheat oven to 400 degrees. Cover a cookie sheet with parchment paper. Mix together sugar, honey, and cayenne pepper. Place bacon on the parchment paper and baste top side with sugar mixture. Bake for 10 minutes. Remove from oven, flip bacon and baste other side. Return to oven for an additional 10 minutes.

Slice of Life

ALL I NEED: REECE & JENNA

Jenna walked through the doorway of The Fix on Sixth, paused, then released a long, slow sigh.

Walked?

She hadn't walked through that doorway. She'd left the art of walking behind weeks ago.

No, today Jenna was waddling. With the occasional lapse into teetering thrown in for good measure.

"It's worth it, though," she whispered, her hand rubbing her huge belly. "Even if you are the reason I can't see my ankles."

She was rewarded with a solid kick, and she jumped, then laughed out loud. Nearby, a hipster couple exchanged a *beware the crazy pregnant woman* glance.

She ignored them, then hurried in a waddling sort of way toward Amanda, who was sitting at the bar chatting with Eric Shay, a wickedly hot bartender who'd somehow managed to avoid being an entrant in the Man of the Month calendar contest.

"Hey, Jenna," he called. "What's your pleasure? Sparkling Pineapple or Bloody Mary with Candied Bacon?"

Amanda's eyebrows shot up to her hairline. "She can't drink! She's pregnant! Or are you trying to get her drunk enough that she'll let us roll her across the room like a bowling ball?"

"You're a hoot," Jenna said, scowling at the bar stool. No way could she get her almost thirty-seven weeks pregnant tush up that high.

"That's me." Amanda winked at Eric. "Providing nightly entertainment to the masses."

"Nightly?" Eric shot back. "I'm pretty sure the only one you're entertaining after dark is Derek."

"Zing!" Jenna teased. Amanda, however, just smiled happily. After years of remaining stubbornly single, she was now firmly rooted in the land of coupledom.

"What about you?" Amanda's attention focused on Eric. "Anything cooking in your relationship repertoire?"

Jenna thrust out a foot, kicking Amanda's shin. For months, Jenna had been trying to push Eric closer to Tiffany Russell, a waitress who Jenna happened to know had a crush on the bartender. But matchmaking was a delicate game, and in this case it was made trickier by the fact that Tiffany used to date Eric's older brother. Any and all relationship maneuvers required chess-like planning and careful deliberation, and Amanda had all the subtlety and finesse of a sledgehammer.

A red flush crept up Eric's neck. "Nothing really." He cleared his throat, then looked straight at Jenna. "Go with the Bloody Mary. I don't have any pineapples prepped."

"Throw in some extra candied bacon, and you've got a deal."

"You got it."

The Bloody Mary recipe was unique to The Fix, and it was excellent even without vodka. But what really made the drink rock was the candied bacon garnish that Tyree, owner and chef, had created. It was like a little strip of heaven in your mouth, washed down with a splash of ambrosia.

"Go have a seat," Eric ordered, nodding at a table. "I'll bring it out to you."

"And that's why we keep you around," she teased, making him laugh. Technically, Jenna was one of four owners of The Fix, along with the original owner, Tyree, her best friend Brent, and her other best friend-turned-husband, Reece.

Not that she'd ever presume to hire or fire a bartender. Her bailiwick was marketing. And ever since the Man of the Month campaign had reached its successful conclusion, she was feeling more than a little at loose ends.

The contest had wrapped in October, and Jenna and her team had rushed to get calendars printed, the pre-sold inventory shipped, and the open inventory stocked in the bar and other local businesses. They'd been simultaneously working on a cookbook filled with Tyree's amazing recipes, and now both *Bar Bites* and the Man of the Month calendar graced the retail shelves of many an Austin boutique.

But both projects had wrapped by mid-December. Then she'd been occupied with her first Christmas as a married woman—*that* reality still made her giddy—and now here she was. The second day of January. A brand new year.

And she didn't have a single idea what to do with herself.

Sure, she could whip up some flyers to promote the bar. Maybe coordinate drink specials or arrange special events surrounding some of the live bands. But the Man of the Month contest had been her brainchild, and it had turned into a big deal. A citywide event. Something that folks talked about on social media and chatted about with their friends. The guys—winners and contestants—were recognized around the town. All in all, it had been a triumph.

And she had absolutely no idea how she was supposed to follow her own success.

"What's with you?" Amanda asked as they settled in at one of the two-tops near the bar. "You've gone from perky to pensive. Something wrong? Or is it hormones? I know it's not Reece."

At the mention of his name, Jenna's mood lifted. "No," she agreed. "Not a thing wrong there. Right, peanut? Your daddy's pretty much perfect." She smiled down at her belly, and when she looked up, a minor miracle took place. Not only did Eric deliver her drink that very second, but Reece stepped out of the back hallway and entered the bar at the far end of the room.

He was yards and yards away from her, but it didn't matter. Even across the cavernous bar—even despite the happy hour crowd that filled the room and kept blocking him from her sight—even then, she could feel him. Could sense him.

The heat of him. The power. The strength…and the tenderness.

With his shaved head, shadowy beard, broad shoulders, and rock hard muscles, Reece Walker was the kind of man who never lacked for attention. Add in the intricate tats that covered his chest, back, and arms—today only visible emerging from the short sleeves of his T-shirt—and he radiated a dangerous sex appeal, like a bad boy biker on a mission to ravage a woman.

Her whole body tightened in response to that particular thought, and as she rubbed her hand over her belly, Technicolor memories of the reason she was in this particular state filled her mind, making her breasts ache and her sex throb with such an intense need that she squirmed on the chair, disguising the sudden, demanding sexual craving by reaching for another piece of candied bacon.

The pregnancy hormones were doing a number on her; she was certain of that. She was ridiculously horny all the time. A little fact that really hadn't bothered her husband one bit.

But this wasn't a hormone reaction. This was a *Reece* reaction. The man called to her without saying a word. Possessed her without using his hands. Captured her with only his eyes.

They'd started out as best friends, and thank God they still fit that definition. But they were so much more.

"Hey, Beautiful," he said, reaching for her. With one hand, he pulled her to her feet. The other he spread wide over her belly. "I missed you both."

Warmth and love spread through her, and she laughed lightly. "I've only been gone a few hours." She'd cut out that morning to go check on the various retailers stocking the calendar and to talk with the printer about a second print run since sales were so high.

"That's a few too long."

"You two have crossed the line from sappy to downright gooey," Amanda said, her lips twitching with amusement. "You know that, right?"

"I've seen you with Derek," Jenna countered. "I'd say you two are contenders for the title in the sappy and gooey department."

"Nothing wrong with sappy," Reece said. And before either Jenna or Amanda could answer, he pulled Jenna close. Her very pregnant belly pressed against his tight, firm body as his arm curled around her non-existent waist to hold her steady. And then, with a passion that made her knees go weak, his mouth claimed hers, hot and wild, and full of demand and promise.

"Wow," she said when he slowly drew back. "What was that for?"

"A preview," he said. "Come on, baby. I'm taking you home."

"You're being unfair, you know," Jenna complained as Reece maneuvered their shiny new-to-them Volvo into the driveway of Reece's father's home. She missed driving her 1972 El Camino that Reece had fixed up for her almost as much as she missed Blue, his restored Chevy truck. But about five minutes into her fourth trimester, Reece had dragged her to a car lot, insisting that they have a newer, safer car now that they had the baby to think about.

She'd burst into tears—damn hormones—and blubbered about how much she loved him for taking care of her and the baby.

As for the other cars… Well, she'd fit behind the wheel eventually.

Now, Reece parked the Volvo next to Blue, then turned to face her, his brow furrowed. "Unfair?"

"A kiss like that, an announcement that we're going home—honestly, Reece, I'm so on edge right now I'd straddle you in the driver's seat and fuck you silly, except for the fact that I can't fit behind the wheel."

"Christ, Jenna…" The heat in his voice was unmistakable, and it curled through her, soaking her panties and making her already aching breasts tighten with a wild, demanding need.

"Yeah, well, I didn't want it to be just me that was suffering. You were at Dr. Blake's this morning, too. No more sex, remember?" Apparently semen could induce labor. And her doctor wanted her to make it full term.

A devious grin slid over Reece's mouth. "I was there. And I talked with Dr. B while you were getting dressed."

"And?"

"And I'm taking you inside."

She frowned, confused. But she also wanted out of the car. So she let him come around to get the door, and then they headed into the house.

For years, Reece had been living in the apartment above the garage, and she'd moved in when they got together. Small but cozy, the place was perfect for two. It would be a little bit crowded with an infant, but they'd make do, and Jenna did love the place. Reece had refurbished it, and the interior gleamed.

Not that they were staying in the apartment now. For the last month, Reece and Jenna had been living inside Charlie and Enid Walker's house, simply because the stairs to the apartment were steep, and she was getting winded and light-headed every time she climbed them. Fortunately, Charlie and his girlfriend, Enid, had gone to Vegas to tie the knot, then they were driving to California to go to Disneyland, Monterrey, and San Francisco.

They promised they'd be back by the time the baby was born, but until then, Jenna and Reece had the house to themselves. They'd entered through the kitchen, and now they moved to the guest bedroom—a room that used to be Reece's when he was a teen, and where Jenna and Brent had spent many hours hanging out with Reece, listening to music, and talking their way through all the world's problems.

At the moment, Jenna's only problem was the fact that Reece wasn't touching her—and the fact that doctor's orders meant that he couldn't touch her the way she wanted. "You're mean for teasing me, you know," she said. "Somehow, I'm going to extract my revenge."

"Hold that thought," he said, then he stepped closer to her and with slow, deliberate movements, he pushed her coat off her shoulders, letting it fall carelessly to the floor. She hadn't buttoned it—for January, it wasn't that cold, and lately she was running so hot that the winter air felt good against her skin.

She was hot now, too, but in a different sort of way. Hot and itchy and so keenly needy that she actually had to fight to keep from whimpering. "Reece," she whispered. "Please. We can't."

"Oh, but we can." His fingers moved to the buttons of her shirt as his lips teased at the corner of her mouth, then traced gently along the curve of her jaw before easing down to her neck. Shivers ran through her, following a path of tiny electric threads that connected all of her erogenous zones. Except, dammit, he'd turned her entire body into an erogenous zone, and every touch, every kiss, every caress was making her more and more wet, more and more hungry for him to take her. To fill her.

Now she really did whimper, and she felt his answering smile as his lips brushed the curve of her breast.

"Ree—"

"Hush," he ordered. "No more words. Just close your eyes and let me handle this."

She wanted to protest even as she wanted to submit—and it was submission that won out. She wanted this. Hell, she needed it. To feel his hands on her, his lips against her skin. And when he pushed back the halves of her shirt to bare her to her bra, she moaned from nothing more than the pleasure of the cool air against her overheated skin.

"I love your breasts like this," he said.

"Huge, you mean?"

"Ripe." He met her eyes. "Not that I didn't love the smaller version. Normally, your tits fit perfectly into my hands. But to see you like this, and to know it's because you're going to have our baby. Jenna, I—"

"Kiss me," she demanded, her body—no, her *soul*—craving him. He didn't disappoint, and he pressed hard against her, her belly making the kiss a little more complicated, but no less heated. And as his tongue teased and danced with hers, his nimble fingers went to the very stretchy waistband of her boring-but-comfortable maternity pants.

He slid them down, taking her panties along with them. He broke the kiss so that he could ease down as he undressed her, holding her steady as she slipped out of her shoes and pants.

He stayed there for a moment, kneeling on the floor, his face tilted back to look up at her. The large belly, her heavy breasts still in the less-than-sexy bra. And there was such awe and hunger in his expression that she felt like the most desirable woman on the planet.

"Reece, please. You're making me crazy, but we can't—"

"Take off the bra and get on the bed," he ordered in a tone that brooked no argument.

She did as he told her, trembling when he stretched out beside her, his hands caressing her bare skin, making rocket flares of awareness shoot through her. He was torturing her, no doubt about that, but it was such sweet torture, and right then, she never wanted it to end.

Gently, his hands brushed over her breasts, his fingers teasing her oh-so-sensitive nipples. She gasped a little, arching up as if to escape the overload of sensations the simple touch launched inside her. "Reece," she murmured, but that was the entire thought. He'd filled her head. He was all she felt. It was just her and him and the wonderful things he was doing to her.

After a moment, he shifted. His mouth replaced his hands, his tongue teasing her sensitive nipple as his fingers moved lower, tracing random patterns on her belly. Then lower still, easing around the mound of her belly to settle between her legs. Just the slightest flicker of a finger over her clit, but it was enough to send strands of pure electricity racing between his finger and his mouth, the heat of his touch connecting her from sex to breast, and then branching out to fill her.

"Please," she said, overwhelmed by the sensations. But that was all she could manage. He swirled his tongue around her nipple, and the resulting awareness in her built between her legs, taking her so close to the edge.

She'd never been a woman who could reach orgasm from a man playing with her breasts, but pregnancy had definitely taken her closer to that state, because she was close now, and it was everything she could do not to beg Reece to fuck her, no matter how much she wanted it.

No penetration, Dr. Blake had said. *It could induce an early labor.*

She whimpered, hating how much she wanted what she couldn't have. Her body was so alive right then, and she wanted her husband inside her. But if she couldn't have that…

"Reece, please." Jenna wasn't even sure what she was asking for. More? Release? His body pressed hard against hers?

He didn't give her time to figure it out, though. Instead, he moved his mouth south, trailing gentle kisses over the mound of her pregnancy, his fingers following his lips, reducing every part of her that wasn't already on fire to ashes.

And then—oh, God, and then—he gently lifted her knees as he spread her legs, and before she could even release a startled little gasp, she felt the brush of his beard stubble on her overly sensitive skin. Then his tongue flicking over her clit. And then, *oh, yes,* his mouth closed fully over her and his fingers thrust inside her.

It was wild. Hot. And so damned overwhelming. She wanted to squirm away because it was just too much. She wanted to stay right there, because she wanted more. She wanted to break apart—and, yes, she wanted Reece to put her back together.

And then whatever she wanted was moot, because it was all upon her. Her breasts tightened, and her body stiffened, and starlight poured over her, breaking her open, lifting her up.

She reached for Reece, calling his name, and he took her hand. She squeezed, holding tight to the man she loved, letting him anchor her so she could find her way back after she exploded into the stars.

"Christ, you're incredible," he murmured as she came back down to earth.

A lazy smile flitted across her face. "Me? I was going to say the same thing about you."

The mattress shifted as he moved up beside her, then pushed a lock of hair off her face. "I love you," he said.

"I love you, too." She glanced down at his rock-hard erection now pressing against her hip. "I could get on my knees…"

A slow, teasing grin touched his lips. "You could. But you'd never get up again."

Couldn't argue with that…but even so…

"But I want—" she began, only to be silenced with a kiss.

"Roll over," he ordered, then helped her get settled on her side, hugging the body pillow she'd bought for support.

He pressed up behind her, his body warm against her back. "This is what I want. To fall asleep like this, my cock hard against your ass, and you in my arms."

"Yeah?" Sleep was dragging her under.

He kissed the back of her neck.

"Baby, right now there's nothing on this earth I want more."

Jenna woke to the smell of pancakes, cursed Reece for not waking her earlier so she could change, then decided not to bother. Their only guests were Brent, Elena, and Faith, after all. Considering Brent was the third leg of the Reece-Jenna-Brent friendship, he'd seen her at her best and her worst, and would hardly be shocked by either the messy state of her long red hair or her extremely ratty but completely comfortable terrycloth robe.

As for Elena, well, because she was Tyree's daughter, she'd been practically family from the day she walked through the doors at The Fix. And, Jenna knew, Brent had been attracted to her from that first day, too. Not hard to see why. With her lovely dark skin, wide eyes, and gorgeous cheekbones, Elena Johnson could be working as a model instead of studying to be an urban planner. But while her looks might have attracted Brent, it was her wit and intelligence that had reeled him in.

This was the first time she'd come over for weekend brunch, though. But being with Brent meant that Elena was part of the inner circle now. And Jenna couldn't have been more thrilled.

So surely she'd deal with the bathrobe.

And as for Faith...

"Aunt Jenna!" The six-year-old's squeals echoed through the house, and Jenna laughed as Faith pounded down the long hall from the kitchen to the bedroom, then stopped short before leaping into Jenna's arms.

"Daddy said I couldn't jump," she announced.

"Probably smart of Daddy. Wouldn't want us both to topple over backward. I know I'd never get up."

Faith laughed, then tentatively held out a hand. At Jenna's nod, she pressed it gingerly against Jenna's belly, then squeaked when she was rewarded with a sharp kick.

"She kicked me!" Faith skipped back toward the kitchen, delighted. "Daddy! Elena! She likes me!"

"She might be a he," Elena said. She was scooping Faith up into her lap as Jenna finally waddled into the kitchen. "Hey! Good morning!"

"Someone let me sleep too long." Jenna shot a fake scowl toward Reece, who was busy with the pancakes and bacon.

Brent lifted his head to grin at her, his ripped arms bulging under the white T-shirt. At the moment, those perfect muscles were being put to good use setting the table. "I'm pretty sure that robe's older than you are," he said. "Didn't your mom used to wear it?"

"No comment." Jenna felt a little twinge; her mom was living in Florida now, but had plans to fly out as soon as the baby was born to help. Jenna couldn't wait to see her again. And hopefully, she wouldn't want her robe back.

"Want me to make you a decaf?" Elena asked as Faith wriggled back to the ground.

"Just juice," she said, taking the one on the counter that Reece was pointing to, already poured and ready for her.

"I'm sorry." Faith spoke in the kind of whisper that carried, her little hand tugging on Jenna's robe.

"What are you sorry for, sweetie?" Elena asked as she stood and walked toward Jenna.

Faith's eyes went wide. Out of everyone in the room, Faith was the only one who knew that Jenna was having a girl. Reece had said he wanted to be surprised, but Jenna had wanted to know—although keeping the secret was ridiculously hard, especially since Reece had told her he was hoping for a little girl.

All of their friends had followed Reece's lead, and Jenna had been about to bust with the secret. Then one night she was babysitting Faith and the little girl asked whether the baby would be a boy or a girl.

They'd entered into a secret pact, involving drinking the sparkling light of the stars (Sprite) and eating the core of the earth (crushed Oreos). And then Jenna had told Faith that the baby was a little girl.

Now, Faith looked about to cry.

"She's not supposed to run in Charlie's halls," Jenna explained, flashing a quick smile to Faith as she tapped the end of the little girl's nose. "But she won't do it again, will you?"

"Nope." Faith shook her head, obviously relieved.

"I think you should tell Elena that she should be the one cooking," Jenna said to Faith, mostly to distract the girl.

"I should? But Uncle Reece always cooks."

"He does. But did you know that Elena is cooking with Tyree now? Do you want to watch later?"

"Is Uncle Tyree coming over?"

Brent laughed. "No, Short Stuff. Some other time. But Elena and Tyree sometimes tape it when they're experimenting with recipes. And then they put it on YouTube."

Faith jumped up and down, clapping her hands. "I wanna watch! Can we?"

Jenna caught Elena's eye. "That cool with you?"

"Sure. I make a fool of myself half the time, but it's fun learning to cook with my dad."

"A fool, my ass," Brent retorted. "She's a natural. Which means I'm going to have to go to the gym twice as much."

Elena moved to his side and kissed his cheek. "Don't worry, baby. If your muscles go soft, you still have your sparkling personality."

He pulled her close and bussed her neck, making her squeal. He peeked over her shoulder at Jenna, then winked. "Ticklish," he said. "My secret weapon."

At the oven, Reece chuckled, then ordered them to get a room.

Faith, looking around at the grownups, appeared uncertain as to whether she should be laughing or leaving. Finally, she went to Jenna and tugged on her robe. "Can I go play in the backyard until breakfast?"

"Sure," Jenna said. She glanced at Reece, remembering that his circular saw and other tools were still set up out there from where he was working on Charlie and Enid's bathroom cabinets. A quick, silent conversation passed between them, then Jenna smiled down at Faith again. "Why don't I go with you? Elena, you want to come too? We can leave the guys to their manly kitchen chores."

"I don't know. If we leave, we might miss Brent in an apron."

"Don't worry, sweetheart," Brent shot back. "If you want, I'll wear an apron tonight." He lowered his voice. "*Just* an apron."

Elena blew him a kiss. "Mister, you have a deal."

Once in the backyard, Jenna and Elena sat on the metal glider while Faith headed for the sandbox. "Thanks for having me over. I know weekend breakfast was always sacred for the three of you."

"Are you kidding? You're with Brent now." She tilted her head, trying to read Elena's expression from the side. "I mean, you guys are good, right?"

Elena turned to meet Jenna's gaze head on. "We're perfect," she said, and a wide smile bloomed, the kind designed to tug at Jenna's heart.

Jenna took her hand and squeezed. "I'm so glad," she said, meaning it with all her heart.

"Me, too." Elena leaned back with a sigh, her eyes on Faith. "It's good to be a couple, isn't it?"

"Yeah," Jenna agreed. "It's the absolute best."

Reece parked the Volvo at the edge of the property, but kept the engine running and both hands on the wheel. He had no idea why he was nervous—after all, this was Jenna. His wife, his love, his best friend—but he couldn't deny that right then the last thing he wanted to do was get out of that car.

"Are we parking?" Jenna shifted a little in her seat, but she was so pregnant she couldn't shift too much. "Because honestly, the bed was a lot more comfortable for that kind of activity."

He chuckled, but kept his eyes on her. Damn, but she was lovely. Her pale skin seemed paler now, and not just because it was winter. He thought she had more freckles, too, and the urge to lean toward her and kiss every one of them was almost overwhelming.

After a moment, she frowned, then reached for his hand. "Reece? What is it?"

Now or never. And honestly, what did he have to be nervous about? She already knew about this plot of land—an entire acre on Lake Austin, just off City Park Road and only minutes from downtown. He'd been holding onto it for years, ever since he'd grabbed it in a foreclosure sale.

What she didn't know was that he wanted to break ground soon. Wanted to build a house. A home. And that he had the plans all made up for exactly that.

"I want to show you something," he said, then told her to wait while he went around the car to open the door for her.

"I hope it's not a picnic," she said. "Because it's a little chilly. And because once I sit down on a blanket, I'm never getting up again."

He laughed, but he could tell by the way she looked at him that the sound was hollow.

"Reece? What's going on?"

"Okay, come here." He took her hand and walked a few yards toward the water. "Kitchen," he said. "Big open windows with a view of the backyard. Fenced, of course, and toddler friendly. And then the bedroom over here," he added, leading her toward the right. "Still a view, of course. And from the bathroom, too, with the kind of glass that turns foggy or clear at a punch of a button."

"You've been playing with your house design again."

He nodded, then pulled out his phone. "More than playing." He opened up a picture of blueprints. "One of Amanda's architect friends did a rough elevation for me, along with a floorplan. What do you think?"

She looked from the phone to him and then back to the phone again. "I think it looks amazing. But Reece—" She closed her hand over his upper arm. "I don't want to spoil your dream, but if you're thinking we should do this now… Sweetheart, we can't afford it."

And this was the part that made him nervous. "Actually, we can. *If* that's what we want to use the money for."

"What money?"

"You know The Fix is staying open, obviously."

"Sure."

The bar was fine now, but near the end of the year, it had been touch and go, and for a while, Reece had truly feared that The Fix was going to die a fast, painful death. Now, however, all was well. He had a job he loved, a wife he worshiped, and a baby on the way.

He wanted a house for all of them.

But only if Jenna wanted it, too.

He drew a breath. "Well, Tyree pulled me aside yesterday—Brent, too—and repaid the money we'd put into the partnership. And with that money as a down payment, we could get a mortgage now and build our dream house."

Her lips pressed together before she exhaled slowly. "It's a lot of money. A lot of debt. What if…" She trailed off with a shake of her head.

"What?"

"What if we lose customers? What if the bar starts to go under again? Bodacious is still a huge competition," she added, referring to the downtown Austin location of a corporate chain bar.

"If that happens, then we find other jobs." He lifted her chin so that she was looking in his eyes. "But I want our baby to grow up in a house. Hell, I wish it were already built, but if we start soon, it'll be up within a year. Eighteen months at most. And this is where he or she will learn to walk. Ride a bike. Fish. Swim." He drew a breath. "Baby, I want that."

He saw her throat move as she swallowed. "I do. Oh, God, yes, I do. I'm just—"

"What?"

"Afraid." She looked up at him, her green eyes big and round. He saw the tears fill them, and his heart started to break. He had no idea what it was that was scaring her—motherhood, married life, work, construction—but he didn't care. He would do whatever it took to take that fear from her eyes.

"Of what?" He took her hands in his, his eyes hard on her face.

"Of me. Of screwing up."

His heart twisted a little. "Oh, baby. You're going to be an amazing mom."

Her smile lit her up from the inside. "Damn right I am." She drew a breath. "But I'm not sure about work. The Man of the Month contest did so great. How am I supposed to top that?"

"That's what you're scared of? You don't have to top it."

"I do—or at least I need a campaign. Something to keep it out there. To keep the bar in people's minds. I have to, Reece. Otherwise why do I even have a job?"

He could argue with her, but he didn't. He understood too well what she meant, and he knew Jenna too well to think that she'd be satisfied simply planning flyers for the bar. She needed an event to manage. She needed to not only feel like she was making a difference, she needed to actually make one.

"You'll think of it," he said, then kissed her gently. "When you least expect it, something will come to you. I have nothing but faith in you," he said, the truth coming easily off his lips. "You amaze me every day. You'll amaze me with this, too."

Faith.

Out of everything he said, that was the word that stuck in Jenna's head.

Now, she looked up into Reece's eyes and knew without any doubt that what he said was true. He *did* have faith in her. A hell of a lot more than she had in herself. But that was okay, because so long as he had her back, she could get through anything.

"You really think so?" she asked, even though she knew he really did. It wasn't just words with Reece. He believed in her…just like she believed in him.

"I do," he said, the echo of their wedding vows making her smile.

"I do, too," she said. "And if you think we can make this house work now, then absolutely yes. I want our family to have a home."

Surprise, then relief, then love washed over his face, and she leaned against him as he put an arm around her and they both looked out toward the water. "Big kitchen windows, right?"

"The biggest."

"Is there a balcony off the master bedroom?"

He chuckled. "There will be after the next go-round."

She tilted her head up for a kiss. "You're easy, Mister. I've got you wrapped around my little finger."

"You do," he said, and when he kissed her, it felt like her whole body was opening up, as if she—

"Jenna?"

She could taste her own panic as she felt the liquid stream down her thighs. Terrified, she looked down, but it was clear. Not blood. Clear.

But she wasn't even at thirty-seven weeks yet, and her doctor wanted her to go to term.

"Jenna!"

"My water broke." Her voice was so soft. How could he hear if her voice was so soft? "It's way too early, Reece, but I think my water broke."

"Get in the car. Right now." He was already bustling her in as he talked, his natural need and ability to take care of people and things going in full force.

She settled in, then hugged herself, trying to keep terror from creeping in. Lots of women delivered a few weeks early. Surely it would all be okay.

"It will," he said, obviously reading her mind. "The baby's going to be just fine."

She nodded, and then everything turned to a blur as she concentrated only on hanging on as he whipped the very zippy Volvo in and out of traffic that was, thankfully, light on this early Saturday afternoon.

"It will be okay," he said again, the repetition making her realize that he was nervous, too. "It will. The baby's cooked long enough."

Cooked.

"That's it," she said, taking a deep breath as a contraction wracked her body. "That's perfect."

He tapped his hand impatiently on the steering wheel as they stopped at a light. "What are you talking about?"

"For The Fix. We can do cooking contests. Or people can submit their recipes and Tyree and Elena can make them, and if customers like them, they go on the menu. Or—" She was thinking as she was talking, her spinning thoughts distracting her from her fear. "Or maybe we can talk to the network about doing another show. Like one of those cooking shows and combine that with a taste-off. Tyree puts his recipes up against the competition."

The light changed, and Reece zipped back into traffic. "*This* is what you're thinking of now?"

She grimaced, her body clenching as another contraction rocked through her, but she nodded, too. "Yes, don't you get it?" The contraction passed and she smiled up at him. "I don't know the details yet, but I've got the idea. I've caught it, and I won't let go."

Her smile widened, and she felt positively radiant. Both hands rested on her belly, all her fear fading away. "It's all good now. Everything's going to be just fine."

Reece's heart flipped over in his chest as the nurse handed him the small bundle and he looked down into the face of his perfect little daughter.

He'd been terrified when Jenna's water had broken early, but as soon as she'd made her pronouncement in the car—*everything's going to be just fine*—a weight had lifted from him.

She'd known.

Call it woman's intuition, a bit of mommy wisdom, or just a lucky guess, but she'd known. And thank God for that.

Reece just wished he'd realized it sooner. He'd been frantic pulling into the hospital, then kicked himself when he realized he should have called the doctor from the car. But Jenna had been calm, telling him it was all good, and they'd meet their baby soon.

Soon, of course, was a relative term. They'd entered the hospital at almost three on Saturday. It was now just past nine in the morning on Sunday.

All through the day and night, he'd held Jenna's hand, telling her silly stories, encouraging her to breathe, assuring her that he was right there. And all the while making silent bargains with the universe that it really would be okay.

When Dr. Blake showed up and added his thumbs-up to Jenna's assessment, Reece had relaxed a little—then tensed up all over again when he saw the intensity of Jenna actually giving birth. The nurse had told him it was relatively easy compared to some mothers' labors, but Reece hadn't truly felt calm until he'd held his daughter in his arms.

"She's beautiful," he said now to Jenna. "Just as gorgeous as her mother."

"Flatterer." Her smile was wide, but tired. Her long red hair hung in limp strands around her face. Her eyes were bloodshot and shadowed with dark circles. None of that registered, though. As far as Reece was concerned, she glowed.

Reluctantly, he passed the swaddled little girl to Jenna, then sat on the edge of the bed so that he could slide an arm around his wife as they both gazed adoringly at their newborn. "We never picked out a name."

"What do you think of Ami? You know, like Amy's Ice Cream, only spelled with an *I*."

"Isn't that the French word for friend?"

"Yup," she said, leaning her head on his shoulder and twisting a bit to look at him. "All things considered, I thought it was appropriate."

"Yes," he said, looking at the woman who was his best friend, his lover, his wife. And now the mother of his child. "I love you," he said, because he just couldn't hold the words in any longer. "And I think that Ami is the perfect name for our girl."

APRIL
Cobb Deviled Eggs
Highball Caesar
Cashew Chicken Wrap
> Sparkling Pineapple
MAY
Cheeseburger Fries
Southwest Rolls
Pimento Cheese Poppers
> Jalapeño Margarita
UNE
ried Green Tomatoes with
Sriracha Mayo
hilly Cheese Dip with
Mini Pull-Apart Bread
BBQ Bacon Chicken Pineapple Kebabs
> Fizzy Watermelon
SLICE OF LIFE
One More Night:
Nolan & Shelby

Cobb Deviled Eggs

7 hard-boiled eggs (most trays call for 12 halves and you always want a backup in case of tearing)

½ cup mayonnaise

2 tablespoons Dijon mustard

½ cup avocado

1 teaspoon salt

1 teaspoon pepper

4 ounces crumbled blue cheese

2 slices bacon, cooked and crumbled

Slice eggs in half and remove yolks. Place yolks in a bowl and mash with a fork. Add mayonnaise, Dijon mustard, avocado, salt and pepper. Mix well and spoon into egg white halves. Top with crumbled blue cheese and bacon.

Highball Caesar

1 bunch romaine lettuce, washed and dried

1 cup freshly grated Parmesan cheese

4 slices bacon, cooked and crumbled

1 cup croutons

1 cup mayonnaise

Juice of 1 lemon (at least ¼ cup)

1 teaspoon Worcestershire sauce

1 teaspoon minced garlic

1 teaspoon anchovy paste

Tear apart lettuce and place in 4 highball glasses. Top with ½ cup Parmesan cheese, bacon crumbles and croutons. Combine remaining ingredients, plus remaining ½ cup Parmesan, in a blender and blend for 1-2 minutes. Pour over lettuce, bacon, Parmesan and croutons.

Cashew Chicken Wrap

1 rotisserie chicken, shredded

¾ cup mayonnaise

1 tablespoon Dijon mustard

1 tablespoon sweet pickle relish

Salt and pepper to taste

4 burrito-sized spinach tortillas

2 cups fresh spinach

4 Roma tomatoes

4 tablespoons Sriracha sauce

1 cup cashew halves

In a large bowl, mix together chicken, mayonnaise, Dijon mustard, relish, salt and pepper to make chicken salad. On one end of each spinach tortilla, layer ¼ cup spinach, ½ cup chicken salad, 1 sliced Roma tomato, 1 tablespoon Sriracha sauce and ¼ cup cashews. Roll and slice in half to serve.

Sparkling Pineapple

1 (46 ounce) bottle pineapple juice

1 cup orange juice

1 bottle champagne

4 pineapples, hollowed out (optional)

In a large pitcher, combine pineapple juice and orange juice. Refrigerate until ready to serve. To serve, add bottle of champagne and pour into hollowed out pineapples with straws or serve in champagne glasses.

Cheeseburger Fries

1 (32 ounce) bag frozen crinkle fries

1 pound ground beef

½ cup diced onion

1 teaspoon Montreal steak seasoning

½ cup ketchup

1 tablespoon mustard

¼ cup dill pickle relish

4 slices bacon, cooked and crumbled

1 cup shredded sharp cheddar cheese

Ranch dressing

Preheat oven to 400 degrees. Bake crinkle fries as directed. Cook ground beef and onion with steak seasoning over medium heat in a large skillet until meat is cooked through and onions are tender. Drain and return to skillet. Stir in ketchup, mustard, and relish, and simmer for 1-2 minutes. Pour over crinkle fries on cookie sheet and top with bacon and cheese. Return to oven for 5 more minutes. Remove from oven and serve with ranch dressing.

Southwest Rolls

2 boneless, skinless chicken breasts, cooked and cubed

1 (15 ounce) can drained black beans

1 (15 ounce) can corn

1 (10 ounce) package frozen spinach, thawed and drained

¼ cup diced red bell pepper

¼ cup chopped green onions

1 teaspoon cumin

1 teaspoon chili powder

1 teaspoon cayenne pepper

1 teaspoon salt and pepper

1 cup shredded Colby/Monterey Jack cheese

8 10 burrito size flour tortillas

1 egg, beaten

6-8 cups of oil for frying

Ranch dressing

Mix together first 11 ingredients in a large bowl. Place all of the tortillas on a plate and microwave for 1 minute to soften them for folding. Next, place 2-3 tablespoons of the chicken mixture onto a tortilla and roll like a burrito, folding in both sides. To "seal" the edge, simply brush a small amount of one beaten egg and finish the roll. Place sealed side down on a cookie sheet and repeat with remaining tortillas. Refrigerate overnight for best flavor. Heat oil to 350 degrees and fry the rolls three at a time for about 5 minutes, or until golden brown. Drain rolls on paper towels, then slice and serve with ranch dressing.

Pimento Cheese Poppers

1 (4 ounce) jar diced pimentos, not drained
8 ounces shredded sharp yellow cheddar
8 ounces shredded sharp white cheddar
1 tablespoon garlic powder
1 cup mayonnaise
8-10 jalapenos, seeded and halved
1 cup flour
2 eggs
½ cup milk
2 cups panko bread crumbs
4 cups oil, for frying

Mix first 5 ingredients together in a medium bowl. Stuff 1 tablespoon of pimento cheese in each half of a jalapeno. Roll each stuffed jalapeno in flour and place on a cookie sheet. Freeze for at least 30 minutes to 1 hour. While the peppers are freezing, whisk together eggs and milk in one bowl and pour panko breadcrumbs in another bowl. Heat oil to 350 degrees in a Dutch oven. While oil is heating, remove peppers from freezer and dredge in the egg mixture and then in panko. Place 3-4 jalapenos at a time in oil and fry for 1-2 minutes. Remove and drain on paper towels. Repeat with remaining peppers.

Jalapeño Margarita

4 ounces Patron tequila

2 ounces triple sec

Juice of 1 lime

4 slices fresh jalapeño

Salt

Wet the rim of a margarita glass and dip into salt. Fill glass with ice. Place tequila, triple sec, and lime juice in a cocktail shaker with 3-4 cubes of ice and shake until well blended. Pour over ice and serve with the jalapeño slices.

Fried Green Tomatoes with Sriracha Mayo

3-4 cups oil, for frying

1 cup cornmeal

1 cup flour

1 tablespoon Cajun seasoning

2 cups milk

1 egg

4 large green tomatoes

In a large iron skillet, heat oil to 350 degrees over medium high heat. In a large bowl, combine the cornmeal, flour and seasoning. In a separate bowl of the same size, whisk together the milk and egg. Slice each tomato into 4-5 slices that are about 1/4 inch thick. Dredge each slice in the dry mix, then the wet, and again in the dry, coating thoroughly. Place 4 slices at a time in the oil and cook on both sides for 2 minutes each. Drain on paper towels and serve with Sriracho Mayo.

SRIRACHA MAYO

1 cup mayonnaise

2 tablespoons Sriracha sauce

1 teaspoon lemon juice

Combine all the ingredients in a bowl. Refrigerate for 30 minutes before serving.

Philly Cheese Dip with Mini Pull-Apart Bread

1 box frozen Steak-umms

1 sweet onion, diced

1 green bell pepper, diced

1 package of baby bella mushrooms, sliced

1 (8 ounce) package cream cheese

2 tablespoons mayonnaise

1 teaspoon Lawry's Seasoned Salt

2 cups shredded mozzarella cheese

Preheat oven to 350 degrees. Cook steak according to package directions and drain on paper towels. In large bowl, place the steak and the remaining ingredients, except for 1 cup of mozzarella cheese. Spread steak mixture into a 9x9-inch baking dish and top with remaining mozzarella cheese. Bake for 20 minutes. Serve with Mini Pull-Apart Bread.

MINI PULL-APART BREAD

4 bakery sub rolls, uncut

2 sticks melted butter

1 tablespoon minced garlic

½ cup chopped parsley

1 teaspoon salt

2 cups shredded mozzarella cheese

1 cup grated Parmesan cheese

Preheat oven to 350 degrees. Place the sub rolls on a foil-lined cookie sheet, and slice each roll crosswise and lengthwise into 1 inch squares, being careful not to cut all the way through. In a microwave safe bowl, add the butter, garlic, parsley and salt and heat for 2 minutes. Pour the butter mixture evenly over each loaf. Bake for 15 minutes and remove from oven. Now, evenly distribute the 2 cheeses over the rolls, making sure to tuck it in every possible spot for the ultimate bite. Place back in the oven for an additional 15 minutes. Serve hot.

BBQ Bacon Chicken Pineapple Kebabs

4 boneless, skinless chicken breasts, cut into 1 inch chunks

1 teaspoon salt

1 teaspoon pepper

1 pound bacon, cut into 2-3 inch pieces

1 (20 ounce) can pineapple chunks

1 cup BBQ sauce

10-15 kebab sticks, soaked in water

Season chicken with salt and pepper. Thread the skewers as follows: wrap a piece of bacon around one piece of chicken, thread onto skewer, place a pineapple chunk next and repeat this order until the skewer is full. Place all of the kebabs on a baking sheet. Preheat grill to 350 degrees and place the kebabs over indirect heat. Grill for 10-15 minutes, then baste with BBQ sauce on all sides. Place on direct heat and grill for 1-2 minutes. Baste again with BBQ sauce and remove from grill.

Fizzy Watermelon

4 cups watermelon puree

1 bottle chardonnay

4 cups club soda

Combine first two ingredients in a large pitcher. When ready to serve, add club soda.

This can also be served in a hollowed-out watermelon with a spout (available at most party stores) for a party.

TO MAKE WATERMELON PUREE:

Remove seeds from watermelon and cut into large chunks. Place in a blender and process until smooth.

Slice of Life

ONE MORE NIGHT: NOLAN & SHELBY

Shelby looked between her friends, her heart pounding, her entire being desperate for help. "Well?"

"You're going to have to be more specific," Hannah said, her wild blonde curls framing her face. "I mean, just telling us that you think something's going on with Nolan isn't much to work with." Her gaze cut to Celia. "So far I've got nothing. You?"

"Sorry, girlfriend," Celia said. She'd recently dyed her hair red, and she tucked an auburn lock behind her ear. "Nada."

Between the two of them, Shelby felt positively plain. Which sucked, because her long, dark hair was her best feature. And plain or not, Nolan loved to touch it, often twisting a strand around his finger when they were in bed. Even when they were in public. It was a silly habit of his that she'd come to cherish, and her stomach seemed to fall away as she wondered if all of that was going to be gone soon. Had they run their course?

The thought made her almost physically ill, which must have showed, because Celia put her hand over Shelby's.

"Hey, it's going to be okay. You just need to tell us more so that we can help. Then it'll all be fine."

"Will it?" So far all that Shelby had told her friends was that she was afraid there was something off in her relationship with Nolan. Just saying anything more than that made her queasy. But they'd both immediately rallied, and when the workday had ended, they'd left Brandywine Finance & Consulting—Shelby the CPA, Celia the secretary, and Hannah the lawyer—and headed over to The Fix on Sixth in order to drown Shelby's sorrows in alcohol. And maybe to excavate some truth out of her random fears and questions.

"It is absolutely going to be okay," Hannah said, squeezing Shelby's hand. "No matter what happens, you're coming out on top."

Shelby's throat tightened. "So you do think something's wrong."

Hannah rolled her eyes. "You haven't told us enough to think that. I'm just talking about you. You are a strong, capable woman. You can get through anything."

Shelby nodded. She was strong. She was capable. At least that's what she'd believed before she'd met Nolan, with his crazy drive-time radio show and his off-color jokes and his way of making her feel like the most precious thing in the universe.

Now, she wasn't so sure about her strength. Because if there really was trouble between her and Nolan, she didn't think she could survive it.

Celia frowned, studying her. "This is really eating you up. Come on, Shel. Tell us what's going on so that we can actually help you."

"Celia's right," Hannah said. "We need more information. And more drinks." The table was already littered with The Fix's Dirty Martinis with Blue Cheese Stuffed Olives, but Hannah raised her hand, signaling to Tiffany for another round.

Idly, Shelby wondered if the fact that she'd come to learn the name of all the staff at The Fix meant she came here too often, but she pushed the thought away. The Fix had become her and Nolan's regular hangout, and she loved the place and the people who worked there.

The thought brought on a fresh wave of anxiety. What if they broke up? Could she come back here?

"*Shel.*" Hanna put her hand on her arm. "Stop it. Just tell us. What's going on?"

"That's just it," Shelby said. "I don't know. Honestly, I don't even know if I need help." She hoped she didn't. Prayed that this weird distance she was feeling with Nolan either meant nothing or, better, that it was only in her head.

Because as much as Shelby had never expected it to happen, she couldn't deny that she was head-over-heels in love with that man. More, she was getting sucked in deeper and deeper with each passing day. If it turned out that his emotions were moving in the opposite direction…

Oh, God. If that was the case, she really didn't think she'd be able to survive.

Which, of course, was why she'd sent out the email SOS right before the end of the work day.

Calm down.

Right. Good advice. She drew in a deep breath, then released it slowly. "Maybe it's all in my head, right?"

"Well, since we still don't know what it is..."

"I know. I just don't know how to put my finger on it," Shelby admitted.

"Has the sex gone downhill?" Hannah asked, making Shelby's face burn.

"No!" A wild memory of last night ripped through her—Nolan's mouth, his fingers, his cock...

She shivered, then lowered her voice. "Not at all, thank goodness. But it's everything outside the bedroom, you know?"

"Again, *no*. We don't know until you tell us."

"Phone calls he obviously doesn't want me to overhear." He'd actually shifted direction and gone out onto the back porch yesterday. After, he'd said he hadn't seen her, but Shelby was sure he had. Her house—*their* house—didn't exactly have dark shadowy areas. She'd been pretty hard to miss.

"And, he was getting a lot of packages. When I asked him what he was buying, he said nothing important. And then the packages stopped."

Celia and Hannah exchanged glances. "So?"

"*So*, they didn't really stop. He just started having them delivered to the station." Nolan was a drive-time radio host at KIKX. His show was over the top, raunchy fun. And Shelby couldn't think of any reason why he'd need to get packages delivered there. But she knew that he was, because the girl at the front desk called her one day last week when Nolan was out of town at a broadcasting conference. She'd asked if Shelby knew if he needed the package forwarded to the conference or if she should just put it on his desk the way she did with all the others.

"So maybe he watches porn and he's embarrassed to tell you."

"Oh, please." Hannah rolled her eyes. "One, nothing embarrasses Nolan. Have you listened to his show? And two, who orders porn through the mail anymore? That's why we have the internet."

"That means it's bad, right?" Shel asked, looking between the two of them.

"It means he's ordering things," Celia said. "That's *all* it means."

"What else?" Hannah demanded.

"The rest is less concrete. A feeling, you know? Like we'll be watching TV or sitting together reading, and I look over and it's so clear that his mind is somewhere else entirely." She heard the hitch in her voice and felt like a fool, but in the moment, all she ever wanted to do was crawl into his head and see what he was thinking. She felt so insecure, so unbalanced. Because she'd given him her love, and that meant he had the power to hurt her. A power no one else held.

She wanted to believe he understood that; she wanted to trust him. But her fear just kept growing.

And as much as she hoped it was all her imagination, she hated the thought of being *that* girl. The whiney, bitchy girlfriend who saw deceit and cheating around every corner.

Surely he wasn't cheating?

She drew in a deep breath and told herself to calm down. "I don't know," she said after Tiffany arrived with the drinks and then slipped away again. "Maybe it's all in my head."

Celia plucked up the plastic toothpick with the bleu cheese stuffed olive on it and pointed it at Shelby. "Take it from the newly married woman. It's never just in your head. If you think something's going on, it is."

"Oh, God..."

"Jeez, Celia." Hannah glared at Celia across the table.

"*But*," Celia continued, her voice full of purpose, "that doesn't mean the something is bad. Maybe he's having a shitty week at work. Maybe you're just misreading the signs." She popped the olive into her mouth, chewed, then swallowed. "There's only one way to know."

"Yeah?" Shel asked, when Celia didn't go on.

"Oh, come on, Shel. For a woman as smart as you are, you're kind of missing the obvious, aren't you?"

Shelby pushed her glasses up on her nose, then looked between both of her friends, frowning.

Hannah and Celia exchanged glances, and then each took one of her hands and squeezed. "Ask him," Hannah said.

Celia nodded. "Sorry, Shel. But you're never going to know until you ask."

Nolan Wood checked his watch as he glanced around the house. *Shelby's house*. Or it had started out that way anyway. Now it was his, too. Just as much as she was his.

With a shake of his head, he realized he was smiling. Not that he wasn't usually—on the whole, he was a pretty laid-back, happy kinda guy. But since he met Shel, it took a rock solid effort to wipe the smile off his face. His Shelby. His paradox. The buttoned-up woman who'd let a loose cannon like him into her life—and in the process had changed him completely.

They'd been together for months now, but he'd known right away that she was special. And that feeling just kept getting stronger, until sometimes when he was around her he thought he might burst if he couldn't release the pressure.

Then again, that's one reason why he loved his radio show; *that* was one hell of a pressure release, after all.

Although it wasn't quite as good as sex…

The thought seemed to shove him around, and he turned to face the suitcase he'd left by the door. For a second, he frowned. Afraid that maybe he was doing this all wrong.

But it was too late now. He'd already made his decision, his plans, and he was diving in.

He pulled the old-fashioned tape recorder out of his backpack. He'd thought it had a fun vintage flair when he'd found it in the station's dusty storeroom along with a pack of unused cassettes. He'd snagged the device and the tapes, then recorded the message. Now, he put the cued-up cassette into the recorder, checked that the batteries were good, and added a Post-it note to the top. He left the whole thing on her coffee table. All things considered, much better than a printed note.

Then he drew in a nervous breath, grabbed his suitcase, and gave the inside of the house one last, long look.

This was it, he thought as he headed for the door. For better or for worse, everything was about to change.

"Ask him," Shelby said as she walked up the steps to her front porch. "Because that's what a sane, rational, reasonable woman would do. An organized woman. A detail-oriented woman. The kind of woman who gets things done and knows how to handle herself."

Too bad that's not you anymore.

"Maybe you used to be sane and organized and on the ball, but you, Shelby Drake, have completely lost it. How do I know? Because you're talking to yourself."

Argh.

She rolled her eyes at her own mental meltdown, then paused in front of her door. The motion sensor lights that Nolan had insisted on installing clearly illuminated the high security keypad lock, and looking at both made her heart twist a little. He took such good care of her. Surely he wasn't—

She shook her head violently, not even allowing negative thoughts in. Her friends were right—she needed to just ask.

She punched in the code, then slipped into the house. She'd caught an Uber from the bar, and she was still punchy enough that coffee was on the agenda, so she aimed herself toward the kitchen, then stopped short when she passed her couch and her coffee table. *A cassette player?*

Why on earth would Nolan be using a cassette player? He dictated all the time, but he recorded everything electronically so he could upload it as one of his show's effects or as part of one of his riffs.

Then she got a closer look, saw the sticky note, and felt her guts shrivel.

Shel-

Push me, play me.

N

She froze. Part of her wanted to play the tape. Another part wanted to run and hide. But that was stupid. If anything was wrong—if he was, God forbid, leaving her—then he wouldn't tell her by cassette. Would he?

Of course he wouldn't, and she knew she was being stupid. But somehow she couldn't shut off her paranoid brain.

She drew in a deep breath, bent to the table, and jammed her finger on the button marked play.

"Gooooood evening, Shelby!" Nolan's radio voice blasted from the speaker, the sound tinny but clear. "It's sometime after work on a Friday evening, and how late it is depends on how many cocktails you had with the girls."

He was mimicking his drive-time schtick—*Mornings with Wood*—and now he lowered his voice as the Twilight Show theme song played in the background. "Shelby Drake entered her home late one night, a little tipsy, a little off kilter. She expected a lazy evening at home, but that's not what she got. No, because when she crossed that threshold, Shelby entered a new dimension. A dimension of sex. A dimension of pampering. A dimension filled with orgasms beyond belief. That's right, Shelby. I'm your man, baby, and tonight is *An Evening With Wood*."

The background song changed to *Rock You All Night Long,* and it wasn't until the music faded and Nolan's voice returned that she realized she was on the floor, her legs having gone weak with relief.

Yup, the jury was in—she truly was an idiot.

"So go change for the evening—wear a skirt for me, okay?—and then step outside. There'll be a car in the driveway, and your driver knows just where to take you. I'll see you soon. Until then, just use your imagination. But I promise it won't be as good as our reality. Happy anniversary, sweetheart. It's been eight months since our very first night."

Eight months.

Anniversary.

She felt like the biggest fool ever.

Shelby stood, her body already on fire, and her head full of guilt. He'd been quiet and weird, all right. All because he'd been planning this. A special night to celebrate eight months. And wasn't that just like Nolan to pick eight months instead of one year? Anything to stand out.

Guilt that she'd so sadly misjudged him weighed her down, but she pushed it aside. There'd be time for self-recrimination later. Now, she hurried to get ready.

It was January, so she put on boots and an ankle length knit skirt that she coupled with a tank top and a cable knit sweater. A couple of strokes of the brush to her hair, a swish of mouthwash, then a quick touch-up of her make-up. Ready.

She grabbed her purse and coat, yanked open the front door, then gasped when she saw the limo parked in her driveway.

As soon as she stepped onto the porch the driver came around to meet her. He nodded in greeting, then opened the door. She entered, expecting to find Nolan in there, despite the fact that his message had suggested she'd be riding alone. But alone in a limo? Where was the fun in that?

Apparently, the fun was in the bar, because before he shut the door, the driver offered her a drink—then poured her a tall Pinot Punch—the very drink from The Fix that she'd been wasted on the night she'd met Nolan.

A wine, Schnapps, and frozen peach concoction, Shelby had discovered the drink after Cam—one of the bartenders at The Fix—recommended it. Considering it was now on her favorite drinks list and had indirectly led her to the man she loved, Shelby guessed that she really owed Cam a thank you.

She assumed they were going downtown, so she drank her glass quickly, wanting to finish it during the short drive. But then the limo turned and they ended up heading south out of the city. By the time they'd pulled up in front of a stunning stone house on what seemed like endless acres of property, almost forty-five minutes and half the pitcher had gone by the wayside.

If Nolan's plan was to get her drunk, he'd succeeded admirably. And considering how drunk she'd been that first night, they were definitely re-creating their first date. Except then, she'd had to prove she was sober before he'd sleep with her. She'd recited prime numbers, she recalled. And she really, really hoped he didn't care about her sobriety today, because at the moment, she wasn't entirely sure what a prime number even was. So much for all those years studying advanced mathematics.

All she wanted—all she could think about—was his mouth on hers, his hands touching her. She wanted to be naked and stretched out beneath him. Most of all, she wanted to feel him moving inside her.

Naturally, *that* was the moment the driver opened the door, and she squeaked a little, certain that her thoughts were all over her face, whatever natural filter she might normally rely on having been completely obliterated by the mass quantities of alcohol.

She let the driver help her out, then stood a bit at the end of the stone sidewalk. For a moment, she was unsure what to do. Above her, a giant moon provided enough light to reveal the path to the house. Past the wash of light, a blanket of stars hung in the velvet sky that seemed to stretch forever and ever. And suddenly, strangely, Shelby felt very small and very alone.

She almost took a step back toward the limo—but then the front door of the house opened and Nolan stepped onto the porch, and just as quickly as everything had tilted sideways, the world righted itself again. He was there; right there. And everything was fine.

For a moment, he simply looked at her, and she basked in the glow of his love. God, she adored him. He had an athletic build, tall and lean, with muscled arms that could hold her tight. His dark hair accented his pale gray eyes, and he had the kind of long lashes that women envied. He was, in a word, delicious. But at the end of the day, it wasn't Nolan's appearance that had won her heart; instead it was the way he looked at the world. And at her.

Like he was looking at her now. A tiger stalking its prey, and she was so very ready to be devoured.

He didn't say a word as his long strides ate up the sidewalk between them, and he didn't say a word when he reached her. He simply kissed her. Although, honestly, there was nothing simple about that kiss. It burned hot and wild, the kind of kiss that she felt more in her core than on her lips. A full-body kiss that fired her senses and left her gasping and grateful he'd hooked his arm around her waist, otherwise she would have melted onto the ground.

"Hey," he said, sliding his hands inside her coat to cup her ass. "You taste good."

"I taste like Pinot Punch."

"Yes, you do."

"I think you were trying to get me drunk."

"Might have been," he said. "Did you already have a head start with the girls?"

She nodded, the guilt from her fears washing over her again. "I'm sorry."

His eyes widened. "For what?"

"For—for going out with them. Otherwise, I could have been here sooner."

"You're here now." His hands on her rear tightened, and he tugged her close to him until she could feel his erection hard beneath his jeans. She drew in a shuttered breath, wanting to touch him, to feel his hands on hers. She wanted him to take away the chill of her fears and of the cold evening air. And when she met his eyes, she saw that same desire on his face. That same raw, wonderful need.

"Inside," he said, his voice ragged with desire.

"What is this place?"

"Just a little fantasy I whipped up."

She laughed, delighted. But the laughter stopped when they stepped through the front door. The entrance hall opened into a wide living area, and the entire area was flooded in candlelight. Faux LED candles, yes, but the effect was the same. They lined the floor of the entrance hall leading in, and then in the living area they covered every conceivable surface.

"I wanted real candles," he said, "but the rental agreement says no open flame. So I bought boxes and boxes of the LED kind." He swallowed, looking suddenly unsure. "Do you like it?"

"Are you kidding? It's lovely, but why?"

"Isn't it obvious?" he asked. "I wanted to give you a romantic weekend. Well, romantic and… you know, there might be… sex… going on, too." He said the latter in a shocked stage whisper, making her laugh.

"I won't tell if you won't."

He led her to the bedroom, which had even more LED candles surrounding a huge, four-poster bed. An open bottle of wine sat on the side table. And black cords were tied to each post.

Shelby licked her lips, her already over-aware body kicking into a higher gear.

"I want you at my mercy tonight, baby," he said, sliding the coat off her shoulders and letting it fall to the floor.

"I always am," she whispered as she lifted her arms, letting him pull off her sweater, leaving her only in her skirt, tank top, and boots.

He stood back, looking at her. "You're so beautiful."

She met his eyes, and the rush of desire she felt for this man almost knocked her over. She'd never felt particularly beautiful, but she knew he saw her that way. Just like she saw the man beneath the wacky banter. "I love you, Nolan," she said, and saw the answering adoration in his eyes.

Then the corner of his mouth quirked up. "None of that sappy romantic stuff yet. We're starting with wild, baby. We're starting with me undressing you, then making you come like you've never come before." His hands went to the hem of her tank and he pulled it up over her head, revealing her breasts, now heavy with desire, her nipples as hard as stones. "After I make you shatter, then you can tell me you love me."

"Deal," she said, wanting to laugh, but unable to because his hands were on her breasts, and the way his thumbs were slowly teasing her nipples was making her crazy, stealing her breath and muddling her senses.

"Sit," he said, nodding to the bed, then bending to remove her boots when she complied.

She expected him to stand then, but instead, he took one foot in his hand and gently traced the curve. Thankfully, she wasn't ticklish—or maybe she was too turned on to be ticklish? Either way, the sensation didn't make her squirm. At least not in a bad way. Instead, it sent strands of pleasure coursing up her legs until her sex was throbbing and she was certain her panties were soaked.

She wanted him to slide his hands up, to follow the path of her bare leg until his fingers found her core. She wanted to feel him teasing her, she wanted his mouth on her. She craved his touch, his tongue, his cock. So far, though, he wasn't giving any of that to her. And she was just about to find the words to complain about that little oversight when he lifted her leg higher, then bent his mouth and gently licked the tip of her toe.

Oh, holy hell—electricity danced up her leg, teasing her clit, and when he actually took her toe into his mouth and sucked, she arched back as waves of pleasure crested over her, tightening her nipples, settling at her sex. Ripples of pleasure spread through her, not quite an orgasm, but definitely a preview of coming attractions.

"Someone likes that." He'd tugged his mouth free, and she'd felt the tug deep in her core. Now he was kissing his way up her leg. Her calf. The curve of her knee. Her inner thigh.

She heard a little mewling noise, realized it came from her, and spread her legs as far as the skirt would let her. Pretty far, considering the knit stretched.

"Beautiful," he murmured. "But I want to see more. Scoot back. Lie down."

She did as he ordered, then laughed as he bent over her and kissed her bellybutton, just above the waistband of her skirt. But her laughter changed to a much more needy sound when he grasped the band and tugged it down.

"Up," he murmured, and she lifted her hips as he pulled the skirt and her underwear the rest of the way off. "Oh, baby, yes," he said, then drew his tongue all over her sex, from her clit to her core.

"Nolan, please." She wanted him inside her. Wanted her body to feel as full as her heart. Full of *him*.

"Patience, baby," he ordered, then slipped off the bed and peeled off his shirt. She watched, practically salivating. He had a gorgeous body, lean and strong. His sculpted abs and muscled arms showed that he worked out but he wasn't a gym rat. As far as she was concerned, that was perfect.

She waited, wanting to see the rest of him, but he foiled her by moving to the foot of the bed, then tying her ankle to the bedpost.

She bit her lower lip, forcing herself to say nothing as he moved to the other leg, then repeated the process.

With a wicked grin, she slid one hand between her legs and stroked herself, her fingers sliding on her wet, slick flesh and the swollen hood of her clit. She kept her eyes on his face, saw the way a muscle twitched in his cheek. "Maybe you shouldn't tie both my wrists," she whispered. "You like to watch, right?"

"I do indeed," he said, then very gently put his hand over hers. Together, they stroked her, touched her, and then he thrust inside her. One finger each, as she arched up, wanting more than just his fingers—or hers.

"But still…" he said, then took her free hand and bound it to a post. A moment later, he kissed her lightly, then ignored her protests when he took the other hand from her sex and bound that wrist, too.

"Meanie," she teased.

"Oh, I think I can change your mind about that." He shifted position, then kissed his way up her legs until his mouth was hot and demanding on her sex and his hands were sliding up her body to cup her breasts. Whatever smooth, slow strokes had been there when they'd touched her together were gone now. This was rough. Sucking, licking, even biting.

He was taking her high, pushing her to the edge, the intensity of his touch so much more vibrant when she was bound and unable to escape the full onslaught of his touch. So that with every lick of his tongue or scrape of his teeth, his fingers tightened on her nipples, bringing her entire body alive with passion, and there was no escaping the fire he'd sent to ravage through her.

"Nolan," she cried, arching back, silently demanding he suck harder, take her closer. Wanting him to squeeze her nipples. Wanting the pain to balance the pleasure. "Oh, please." She was close, so close, and just a little bit more and she'd reach the edge. She'd go over. And then she'd see the same stars that filled the sky outside the window.

"Tonight, I want to come with you," he said, and even as he spoke, he pulled the cord to release the two slipknots binding her wrists. Then he did the same with her ankles.

"Hurry," she whispered, but she needn't have urged him. He was on top of her almost immediately, their mouths rough and hot together. A primal meeting, with legs twining, hands grasping, fingernails scraping.

He pulled back once, breathing hard, his eyes on fire. "I love you," he said, and the words shot through her, full of passion and power.

"I love you, too. Please, Nolan. I need you now."

"Over." He spoke the word even as he twisted her, urging her onto her hands and knees. "I can't go slow."

"No—God, no."

His hands were on her hips, his cock at her core. "Touch yourself," he demanded. "And touch me."

She did, one hand teasing her clit, her hand positioned so that she could stroke his velvet-hard cock as he pounded into her, filling her. Claiming her. "That's it, baby," he said. "That's it. Now come with me." She could feel how close he was, and when he leaned over her and one hand pinched her nipple, she felt her core spasm around him, heightened when he slipped the finger of his other hand inside her. She was close, too, so close she just needed a little more and then—*Oh, God, yes.*

He'd moved his hand from her pussy to her ass, the slick fingertip sliding in just to a knuckle, and the unfamiliar pressure had pushed her over the edge. She came violently. Deliciously. Her body pumping him, emptying him. Wanting every bit of him, taking everything he gave until, spent, her muscles could no longer support her and she fell onto the bed with Nolan beside her, their legs twined, their faces so close that they were breathing the same air.

"I think you've destroyed me." Shelby stretched, feeling deliciously used. "In the best possible way."

"Good," he said, lazily drawing circles on her bare skin. "Then you're primed for what comes next."

"Next?" She pretended to groan. "Any more and you might have to bring me back from the dead."

He didn't answer. Not at first, anyway. But then he cleared his throat, and he actually sounded nervous.

She shifted so that she could prop herself up on an elbow, but his fingertip moved to her breast, making her close her eyes and bite her lip.

"I talked to your dad—"

Her eyes flew open as she accidentally bit down too hard on her lip, drawing blood. "What?"

"I just—I know I'm not the guy your father wants for you—"

"Dammit, Nolan." She shoved herself up onto her elbows. "You know that doesn't matter to me. We talked—"

"Hush," he said, pressing a finger to her lip. "I believe that it doesn't matter to you. But it matters to me. He doesn't have to love me. He damn sure doesn't have to like what I do for a living. But he needs to know that I love you."

"I—Oh. What did you do?"

His wide smile reminded her of Tom Cruise's cocky grin in that classic movie, *Risky Business*. "I told him."

"Oh. And he was—"

"And I told him something else, too."

"Yeah? What?"

He slid off the bed, then grabbed something from behind one of the candles on the bedside table. She sat up, both because she was confused and because she wanted to see him better. "I told him that I was going to ask you to marry me."

Her breath left her in a *whoosh*, and her heart fluttered wildly in her chest.

He held up a ring, the diamond sparkling in the fake candlelight. "Shelby Drake, I love you more than I ever thought possible. Will you be my wife?"

She nodded, because she couldn't seem to remember how to form words, and it took a while to finally fumble out even a single word. "Yes," she said, sliding off the bed and dropping to her knees in front of him as he slid the ring on her finger. "Of course, yes."

And then, dammit, she burst into tears.

Joy was leaping through Nolan with such intensity that it took a second to process that her tears weren't of the normal newly-engaged variety.

"Shelby?" She was on the floor in front of him now, and he threaded his fingers into her hair, then held her face so that she had no choice but to look at him.

After a moment, she smiled, albeit weakly, then took a shaky breath, obviously working to hold back the tears.

"Hey," he said gently. "What is it? That doesn't look like happy crying to me."

"It is—oh, God, Nolan, it is. It's just that I was so afraid earlier, and now—to be this happy—it's all sort of a head rush."

A wave of cold caught him unaware. "Afraid?"

"The packages," she explained. "And there were phone calls. I thought—Well, I let my imagination run away. I guess I thought you were going to leave me, and I—"

She broke off with a ragged sob that almost shattered him.

"Oh, baby." He pulled her close, then held her tight. "I'm so sorry." God, he was an ass. "I was all about the show. The event. Making my proposal into a big to-do. I never thought—I never—"

She gripped his hand. "*No*. Oh, please, Nolan, don't think that. This is perfect. And my fears—well, I already knew how much I love you, but it wasn't until I thought you might be leaving that I had a sense of how hollow life would be without you. Honestly, I didn't see how I could even get up on a morning when you weren't beside me. I really didn't know if I could do it."

The tears fell again, and he gently brushed them away.

"Oh, baby," he said, still wanting to kick himself for scaring her even a little. "The good news is that you'll never have to find out."

Her wide smile filled his heart to bursting. "Happy anniversary," she said, then kissed him lightly. "But now the gauntlet's been thrown."

He cocked his head, looking at her curiously.

"I just mean that if this is what you pull together for an eight-month anniversary, then what will you manage for our twenty-fifth wedding anniversary?"

"Wait and see, baby," he said, pulling her close. "You're just going to have to wait and see."

JULY

Fried Pickles and Pickled Okra
Catfish Bites with Loaded Hushpuppies
Brisket Sliders
> Blueberry Mint Julep

SLICE OF LIFE
Don't Let Go:
Spencer &
Brooke

AUGUST

Smoked Salmon Dip
Boom Boom Shrimp
Mini Crab Cakes with Lemon Mustard Sauce
> Pinot Punch

SEPTEMBER

Bacon Wrapped Tater Tots
Pretzel Bites with Beer Cheese Dip
Farmhouse Sliders
> Loaded Corona

Fried Pickles and Pickled Okra

Oil for frying

2 (8 ounce) containers sour cream

1 (20 ounce) jar hamburger dill pickle slices, juice reserved

1 cup flour

1 cup cornmeal

2 tablespoons Cajun seasoning

1 (16 ounce) jar pickled okra

In a Dutch oven or deep fryer, bring about 6 cups of oil to 350 degrees. In a small bowl, combine the sour cream with the pickle juice from the jar. Next, mix together the flour, cornmeal and Cajun seasoning in a medium bowl. Dip each piece of okra and pickle slices into the sour cream mixture and then into the dry mixture. Add about 6 pieces at a time to the fryer and cook for 1-2 minutes. Repeat until all okra and pickles have been fried. Drain on paper towels.

Catfish Bites with Loaded Hush Puppies

½ cup mayonnaise

2 cups whole milk

2 cups flour

1 cup cornmeal

¼ cup Cajun seasoning

2 tablespoons garlic powder

Oil for frying

10-12 catfish fillets, cut into 3-inch pieces

Combine mayonnaise and milk in a mixing bowl. In a separate bowl, mix together the flour, cornmeal, Cajun seasoning and garlic powder. In a Dutch oven or deep fryer, bring oil to 350 degrees. Dredge each piece of fish in the wet mixture and then the dry mixture. Place in the oil and fry for about 4-6 minutes until done. Drain on a paper bag and serve immediately.

LOADED HUSH PUPPIES

1 2 lb. bag hush puppy mix (I use House Autry)

1 onion diced

1 (15 ounce) can cream corn

1 (10 ounce) can Rotel

¼ cup pickled jalapenos, diced

1 bottled beer

¼ cup buttermilk

¼ cup milk

6 cups oil, for frying

In a large bowl, combine all ingredients except for oil. Let sit for 15-20 minutes. Heat oil to 350 degrees in a deep fryer or Dutch oven. Drop 1 tablespoon of batter into oil and fry until golden brown, about 1-2 minutes. Fry 4-6 at a time until all batter is used. Drain on paper towels.

Brisket Sliders

Beef Brisket (leftover)
1 onion, thinly sliced
1 cup mushrooms, thinly sliced
4 tablespoons butter
1 tablespoon soy sauce
12 slider potato rolls
½ cup mayonnaise
6-8 slices provolone cheese
1 teaspoon minced garlic
2 tablespoons chopped parsley

Preheat oven to 350 degrees. Shred leftover brisket. In a medium saucepan, sauté onion and mushrooms with 1 tablespoon butter and soy sauce for 5-7 minutes, then set aside. Slice potato rolls in half and spread mayonnaise evenly on each half. Place bottom half of rolls in a 9x9-inch baking dish. Spread brisket to cover bottom half of rolls. Top with onion mixture and provolone cheese. Place tops of rolls on cheese. In a small bowl, melt remaining 3 tablespoons of butter and stir in garlic and parsley. Brush over the top of rolls. Cover with foil and bake for 10 minutes, then remove foil and bake for 2-3 minutes or until golden brown.

BEEF BRISKET

5-6 pound beef brisket
1 cup flour
Salt and pepper to taste
¼ cup oil
1 Vidalia onion, sliced
2 tablespoons minced garlic
¼ cup soy sauce
1 can beef broth
½ cup of white wine
¼ cup honey
1 tablespoon sage

Preheat oven to 350 degrees. Cover brisket in flour and sprinkle with salt and pepper. Heat oil in skillet on medium high heat and sear all sides of the brisket. Place brisket in a roasting pan without the rack. In the same skillet, add the onion and garlic and sauté until onions are tender. Next, add the remaining ingredients and bring to a boil. Allow to simmer for 10 minutes, then pour the mixture over the brisket, cover and bake for 3 hours. Remove brisket from oven and let rest for 30 minutes before slicing. Slice thinly on the bias and place on a platter. Then, pour remaining sauce from the roasting pan into a skillet and cook on medium high until reduced by half. Pour over the brisket for a wonderful dish and beautiful presentation.

Blueberry Mint Julep

1 cup sugar

1 cup water

1 cup blueberries

6 ounces Makers Mark bourbon

Fresh mint

In a small saucepan, over low heat, combine sugar, water and blueberries. Bring to a full boil, stirring constantly, then remove from heat and allow to cool completely. In 4 highball glasses or mint julep cups, add 3-4 ice cubes, 1.5 ounces bourbon and equal parts blueberry syrup to each glass. Garnish with mint sprigs.

Smoked Salmon Dip

16 ounces smoked salmon

8 ounces cream cheese, softened

1 cup sour cream

1 cup mayonnaise

1 cup green onion, chopped

1 teaspoon Worcestershire sauce

1 teaspoon salt

1 teaspoon pepper

Shred smoked salmon with a fork on a cutting board, without skin. In a large bowl, mix together all ingredients and refrigerate for at least 1 hour to overnight. Serve with crackers.

Boom Boom Shrimp

6 cups oil, for frying

1 pound jumbo (16-20 count) shrimp, peeled and deveined

1 cup cornstarch

½ cup mayonnaise

½ cup Thai sweet chili sauce

½ cup green onion

1 bunch romaine lettuce

Heat oil to 350 degrees in a Dutch oven. In a large bowl, dredge shrimp in cornstarch to cover. Fry 5-7 shrimp at a time and drain on paper towels. In a separate bowl, mix together mayonnaise and chili sauce. Toss shrimp in chili mixture and top with green onion. Serve on a bed of romaine lettuce.

Mini Crab Cakes with Lemon Mustard Sauce

1 pound lump crab meat

4 green onions, chopped

1 egg

½ cup plain Greek yogurt

3 cups panko breadcrumbs

1 teaspoon Cajun seasoning

8 tablespoons (1 stick) butter

In a large bowl, combine crab meat, green onion, egg, yogurt, 1 cup panko breadcrumbs and Cajun seasoning. Form into cakes about the size of a half dollar and cover each side with remaining panko breadcrumbs. Place on a cookie sheet and refrigerate for 30 minutes. In a large skillet, heat 1 tablespoon of butter over medium heat. Remove cakes from the refrigerator and pan sear 4-6 at a time, making sure not to overcrowd the pan. Brown on both sides for about 2-3 minutes or until golden brown. Serve with Lemon Mustard Sauce.

LEMON MUSTARD SAUCE

4 tablespoons mayonnaise

2 tablespoons whole grain mustard

Juice of 1 lemon

Combine all ingredients and refrigerate for 30 minutes or longer.

Pinot Punch

1 (1.5 Liter) bottle Pinot Grigio

½ cup peach schnapps

½ cup orange juice

1 bag frozen sliced peaches

1 liter Sprite

Mix first four ingredients together in a large pitcher and refrigerate for 1 hour. Add Sprite and serve.

Bacon Wrapped Tater Tots

8 ounces sour cream

1 tablespoon ranch seasoning

1 pound sliced bacon

1 (32 ounce) bag frozen tater tots

Preheat oven to 400 degrees. Mix together the sour cream and ranch seasoning and set aside. Cut bacon slices into thirds and wrap around each tot. Place on a cookie sheet (with sides). Bake for 20 minutes, remove from oven and place on a serving platter. Place the sour cream mixture in a resealable bag and cut one corner off. Pipe over tots and enjoy!

Pretzel Bites with Beer Cheese Dip

1 (11 ounce) tube refrigerated pizza dough

4 cups of water

¼ cup baking soda

2 eggs, beaten

4 tablespoons sea salt

4 tablespoons butter

½ cup flour

1 (12 ounce) bottle of beer

4 cups shredded extra sharp cheddar cheese

8 ounces cream cheese

2 teaspoons salt

1 teaspoon pepper

1 teaspoon garlic powder

1 teaspoon onion powder

Preheat oven to 425. Roll out dough and cut into 1-inch strips, then cut each strip in half. Tie each strip into a knot. Bring water and baking soda to a boil and drop 8-10 dough knots at a time into the water for 30 seconds, then transfer to a greased 9-inch pie pan, lining the outside edge of the pie pan. Next, brush each one with the egg wash and top with sea salt. In a medium skillet, melt butter over low heat and stir in flour until a roux forms. Slowly stir in beer and mix until sauce thickens. Add both cheeses and continue to stir until sauce is smooth. Pour into center of pie pan with uncooked pretzels and bake for 15-20 minutes or until golden brown and bubbly. Serve immediately.

Farmhouse Sliders

2-3 tablespoons butter
1 onion, thinly sliced
2 teaspoons soy sauce
1 pound ground beef
½ cup mayonnaise
12 slices extra sharp cheddar cheese
1 teaspoon minced garlic
12 small eggs
Salt and pepper to taste
2 teaspoons Montreal steak seasoning
12 slider potato buns
12 slices bacon, cooked and drained

In a large skillet over medium heat, melt 1 tablespoon butter and add onion and soy sauce. Sauté until translucent, about 3-5 minutes. Remove from heat and set aside. In a large bowl, combine ground beef and Montreal steak seasoning. Form into 2-inch patties. Preheat grill to medium and cook burgers for 5-7 minutes, turning halfway through, or until 160 degrees for medium (170 degrees for well done). In a small bowl, combine mayonnaise and garlic. Using the same skillet as before, over low heat, melt ½ tablespoon butter and crack 4 eggs into skillet, making sure to keep separated. Salt and pepper eggs and flip after 1 minute. Continue to cook for an additional 30 seconds to 1 minute and immediately remove from heat for an over easy egg. To build each slider: spread 1 tablespoon of garlic mayonnaise on slider bun, top with beef patty, 1 slice cheddar cheese, 1 tablespoon sautéed onion, 1 bacon slice and 1 egg. Repeat for the remaining 11 sliders.

Loaded Corona

12 pack Corona

1 pint rum

2 limes, sliced

salt

Pour out the "neck" of each Corona and replace with rum. Roll each slice of lime in salt and place in the top of the corona. Serve.

Slice of Life

DON'T LET GO: SPENCER & BROOKE

Brooke Hamlin had always known that the historic Drysdale Mansion came with ghosts… She just wished that for once she could enjoy an afternoon without them.

The ghosts in question were Casper (as in "The Friendly") and Nick (as in "Nearly Headless") and neither of them were really ghosts, of course. Instead, they were the cameramen for the reality show that Brooke and her fiancé, Spencer, were currently starring in—*Mansion Makeover.*

Those, of course, weren't their real names, but since they were supposed to be invisible, Brooke and Spencer's former intern had given them the nicknames back when they were filming *The Business Plan,* which had finished its network run in October to fabulous reviews.

The same cameramen had followed them from the renovation show based at The Fix on Sixth to the current show they were filming, right here at the Drysdale Mansion, which also happened to be Brooke and Spencer's home.

Which meant she could never escape the ghosts. Not ever.

They were here during the days. They often lingered at night.

Tomorrow they'd be lurking about during their engagement party. A staged event that Spencer and Brooke hadn't even wanted—not like this, anyway. They'd just wanted to *be* engaged. Maybe have a few drinks with their friends at The Fix.

Instead, the show insisted on having The Fix cater a huge party at the mansion for everybody they'd met. The idea, of course, was drama—as if their remodeling show was a spin-off of *The Real Housewives* franchise, and not a real property show meant to be entertaining, educational and endearing.

The whole situation annoyed her, and it was something she hadn't anticipated when they'd been doing on-camera renovations at The Fix. Then, the schedule had been much more set, and the focus was as much on the bar and the calendar contest as it was on her and Spencer.

Here, it was all about the house. And the cameras had become a constant in their lives.

In her heart, she knew it was a blessing. After all, there was no way that she and Spencer could afford the mansion otherwise, and this incredible, historic house represented Spencer's dream. For years, he'd wanted to not only bring it back to its full glory, but to claim the historic building as his own. *Mansion Makeover* had given him the chance. But only because the network was subsidizing the costs of renovations.

And that, of course, made living under a microscope all worthwhile.

Really.

Or, mostly.

Or, maybe?

The truth was, she hated it. Living like this. In a permanent spotlight where every little thing was filmed. Every. Little. Thing.

Lately, about the only privacy she and Spencer had was in the bedroom, and she wouldn't be at all surprised if Molly and Adam, their producers, insisted that the ghosts live quietly in the corner. After all, nothing spelled ratings better than S.E.X.

"You ready, Brooke?" A recent graduate from the theater department at the University of Texas, Taylor D'Angelo had stage managed the calendar guy contest last year at The Fix on Sixth. She and Brooke had gotten to know each other pretty well, and when the contest had wrapped, Taylor had approached Brooke about working on their new reality show. One thing had led to another, and now Taylor was working as *Mansion Makeover's* Second Assistant Director.

The show was designed in such a way that part of it was "fly on the wall," with the camera simply recording the work and conversations between Brooke, Spencer, and their renovation crew. The rest consisted of demonstrations of specific projects or skills, and in those segments Brooke or Spencer—often the two of them together—would demonstrate the process and talk to the camera at the same time.

Today, Brooke was doing a demonstration while Spencer ran to Home Depot to get a few more supplies. Specifically, Brooke was tiling the sunroom, which had been prepped down to the concrete a few episodes ago.

"Ready when you are," she said to Taylor after the crew had done a quick touchup of her makeup. They didn't call "Action" since this was reality TV and the producers wanted the footage to feel as raw and real as semi-staged television could feel. Which meant that Brooke could jump in whenever she wanted, which she did now by smiling at the camera.

"As you can see by the boxes, we're going to be working on tiling the sunroom today." She started toward the corner, where a stack of tile waited. "The first question you face in a room like this is what type of flooring to go with. In this case, we wanted to stick as close to the original as possible, which is why we're going to be redoing the flooring of the sunroom in—*shit!*"

The curse came a split second after the stumble, and Brooke found herself on hands and knees on the rough concrete subfloor, her jeans ripped, and her ego bruised. "Dammit!" And then, as Casper took a step closer, his camera aimed right at her, she snapped, "Turn that thing off!"

His eyes widened. She felt like a jerk and a klutz and a loser all rolled together into one big, completely stressed-out ball.

And then, without warning, she burst into tears.

"Brooke!" Taylor's concerned voice cut through the thrum of emotion in her head. But it wasn't until she heard the familiar tread hurrying toward her that she felt her body relax, finally going slack when Spencer knelt behind her and wrapped her in his arms.

"Brooke? Brooke, baby, what's going on?"

She felt him lift his hand off of her arm, and she opened her eyes in time to see Taylor nod at some signal Spencer had given her. Then Taylor ushered everyone out.

"They're gone, Angel," Spencer said, releasing her. He stood, then moved in front of her, and she looked up into his warm, dark eyes. How often had she looked deep into him? How many times had his strong hands caressed and soothed her? How many times had his beard scratched her when he held her close and kissed her with such passion it made her knees go weak?

Spencer Dean knew her better than anyone in the world, and in that moment, she knew that she didn't have to explain. He got it. More important, he got *her.*

He reached down and she put her hands in his, relishing the comfort of their connection as he tugged her gently to her feet. "They're gone," he repeated. "At least for now. And I'm so, so sorry."

It was that apology that finally got her mind humming again. That, and the simple fact that having him beside her had sent relief coursing through her with so much power that she didn't have any room left inside her for the irritation and frustration.

"You don't have anything to apologize for," she said. "I'm the one who lost it." She released his hands and dragged her fingers through her long, blond hair. "I tripped over my own damn feet and everything inside me just exploded, but it's not your fault."

"Isn't it?" He cocked his head toward the den, then pressed his palm gently against her back and steered her off the sunporch and into the house proper. She sat on the sofa they'd picked out two episodes ago. This was the first room to be fully finished, and as she settled back against the thick, comfortable cushions, she looked up at the high, tiled ceiling and the restored period molding. Not a detail had been ignored, and the room was a showplace now. And she and Spencer owed that to the television program as much to their own hard work and planning.

She drew in a long breath, then released it again. "No," she said firmly. "It's not your fault."

"I'm the one who pushed for *Mansion Makeover*. I'm the one who made this show happen." He sat down next to her, his thigh hard against hers. Then took her hand and twined their fingers together. She squeezed, relishing this connection to him. The man she loved. The man she'd lost once, but had miraculously regained.

"I want it, too," she said. "I love this place." The historic mansion had been stunning even in its dilapidated state, and slowly but surely they were bringing it back to life. It was work she loved with a man she loved. There was just that one little hitch. "It's only…it's just…I mean, I guess I finally reached my limit of being under the microscope. I don't normally mind—I really don't. I knew what I signed on for when I agreed to do the show with you. But they're here all the time. And tomorrow—our engagement party? Except it isn't even really our party because it was *their* idea. Molly and Adam's."

She sucked in another breath and leaned against him. "I know I sound whiney and ungrateful considering that once it's over we're going to have this incredible home. It's just that every time I turn around it feels like someone from the production is behind me."

"I get it," he said, brushing his thumb along the curve of her jaw, the contact sending shivers through her. "I really do."

Slowly, he kissed her. His mouth firm against hers. Tender at first, then with rising heat, until the ache inside her consumed her, so that she gasped with love and longing when he pulled away, his eyes shining with need.

"And Angel," he said, "they're not here now."

Spencer had never felt more powerless in his life. More than that, despite her protests, he knew damn well that he was the source of her frustration. Not him, but his plan to finance the renovation by pimping them both out to the show. He'd gotten them into this, she was hating it, and by default, she should probably hate him.

She didn't, though.

If he didn't already know how much she loved him—and that was one of the most incredible truths of his life—he would have been able to tell simply from the expression of love and joy that colored her face right now. Not to mention the slow, sexy grin that touched her lips as she processed his words.

"You're right," she said, her voice husky. "They really are gone." She reached for the collar of his T-shirt, then fisted her hand in it as she pulled him closer, her lips brushing his as she spoke. "Make love to me, Spencer. Right here on this couch, because for the first time in a long time, there isn't a single damn camera in this room."

Her words shot through him. Her bold, demanding touch fired his blood. He'd already been half-hard just from having her in his arms, but he'd been hesitant, too, knowing she was upset and that she'd fallen.

She'd just swept away the last cobweb of uncertainty, though. Her need was so palpable it seemed to reach out and grab him, then mingle with his own luminous desire, a feeling so intense it lingered over them like pulsing neon. *Now. Finally. Alone.*

God, yes.

Without another word, he claimed her mouth. Not a polite kiss, but raw and hard, with tongue and teeth and wild abandon. And the real joy of it was in the way she kissed him back, opening herself to him. Giving her entire body to him the same way that she'd given her heart—open and freely and completely.

She shifted, then pulled her legs up onto the couch. He knew her well enough to anticipate her move, and gave her space to get settled before straddling her, roughly yanking the sofa's cushions out of place and tossing them over the back.

Her laugh delighted him, but that didn't keep him from silencing her with a fresh kiss. This one, however, he broke quickly. "I want to see you naked," he said, delighted when the humor in her eyes faded to heat.

She said nothing in response, but she shifted onto her elbows, then pulled her shirt over her head and tossed it aside. Then her fingers reached for the button of her jeans. He stilled her motion with his hand, wanting to do it himself. Even after all these months—even after slipping the engagement ring on her finger—there were still moments when Spencer couldn't believe the universe had righted itself and she was now really and truly his.

Slowly, he unzipped her jeans, then pulled them down over her hips. He paused long enough to trace a fingertip along the band of her panties, then held his breath as he watched the tightening of her muscles, as he heard the small gasping sound she made before stifling it by putting a knuckle into her mouth and biting down in a way that made his cock twitch with the memory of all the times she'd sucked him dry.

"Angel," he murmured, forcing himself to continue until finally he'd tossed aside her slip-on sneakers and tugged her jeans over her ankles and feet. He dropped them negligently on the floor, then spread her legs slowly, his eyes on hers.

"Spencer, please."

The words were simple; the heat in them was much more complicated. She was ready—he knew the signs so intimately now. The way her skin tightened. The soft sounds of arousal that worked a kind of magic on him. And the scent of her, a primal, sexual musk that almost demanded he sink deep inside her, taking them both to places they'd never manage on their own.

So yes, she was ready...but he was going to make her wait.

First he wanted to taste her, wanted to drive her crazy. Wanted to hear this woman he loved—this beautiful angel who would soon be his wife—beg for mercy before he fucked her hard. He'd claimed her so many times already, but there was never enough. Could never be enough. And with one quick, brutal motion, he tightened his grip on her thighs, then pulled her roughly toward him, lifting her hips and hooking her legs over his shoulders as he knelt between her legs, then closed his mouth over the thin strip of damp silk that covered her pussy.

He sucked her through the silk, relishing the way she arched up, her ankles locking behind his head. He jerked her higher, wanting her tighter against his mouth as he sucked and licked, then ran his tongue along the line of her panties between her sex and her thigh. She squirmed, she begged, and still he didn't relent.

Until finally, he couldn't take it any more and he used his teeth to tug her panties aside, losing himself in the taste of her as he thrust his tongue deep inside her warm, wet folds.

"Please," she murmured, as one hand closed over a breast and the other slid between her legs. Her finger brushed his tongue as she teased her clit, her core tightening and throbbing. She was close—He knew she was so damn close, but he wasn't about to let her explode. Not yet. Not until he was inside her.

He pushed back, making her cry out in surprise and then prop herself up on her elbows as he violently ripped his shirt free from his jeans, then started to pull it over his head.

"No," she said, reaching for him.

He paused, meeting her eyes, certain she didn't mean to stop.

"I want you dressed." She shifted on the couch, managing an almost acrobatic maneuver that ended with her on her knees beside him. Her fingers reached for his fly. He understood what she wanted and let her free his cock before he leaned back against the one remaining cushion, fully dressed except for his erection, now freed from confinement and eager for her.

"Stand up," he ordered, and she did. His beautiful fiancée, his naked angel. His heart flipped over once again as that single word played in his head once more—*His.*

How the hell had he gotten so lucky?

He met her eyes and knew what she wanted. What he wanted, too.

"Come here, Angel," he said. "Come ride me."

Come ride me.

Those were the words Brooke heard, but they meant so much more. They meant *You're mine.* They meant *I'll protect you.*

Most of all, they meant *I love you.*

And oh, dear God, she loved him, too. Loved the way he looked at her. The way he cherished her. The way he understood her. Hadn't he cleared out the house? Hadn't he given her this night?

Now she gave herself to him. Only not really, because she'd done that long ago. She belonged to Spencer, body and soul, and the engagement ring she wore proved it.

Slowly, because she wanted the moment, she straddled him, using her thigh muscles to keep her sex barely over the tip of his cock. His jeans rubbed her inner thighs by her knees and she smiled. There was something so delicious about being naked and making love to a fully dressed man. It made her feel possessed. Owned. Something she wouldn't want with anyone but Spencer, but with him, it was as fundamental as breath. As essential as blood.

He started to reach for her breasts, but she shook her head. "Hold my hips," she ordered, enjoying being the one in charge.

With one hand, she cupped his head, the other pressed against his abs, so tight from both his gym routine and the manual labor of their job. She kept her eyes open, then moved her hips—small motions that stroked and teased the head of his cock. It was a maneuver designed to drive him crazy, and she knew she'd succeeded when she saw his eyes go glassy.

A trill of victory shot through her, but it was as much his victory as hers, because as she'd teased him, she'd also been torturing herself. Now, her core throbbed, craving his cock. Her breasts ached, her skin tingled all over, and her clit felt so swollen and sensitive that a tiny breeze would undoubtedly send her rocketing off into space.

That was it; she couldn't wait any longer.

She shifted her hands to his shoulders for balance, then wiggled her hips until his steel-hard cock was right at her core. Their eyes met, and she lowered herself just enough to draw the head of his cock into her. Heat flared in his eyes, making her even more wet, and when he slid his finger up and down her perineum, she couldn't take it any more. She thrust herself down on him, his cock filling her core as his fingertip rimmed her ass. He arched back, his hand still on her hip, helping guide her as she rode him hard, lost in the storm of sensations, all merging together now to push her over the edge.

"Come with me." His voice, though clearly an order, came out raw, giving her all the power. All the control. And that, frankly, was erotic enough to send the first shudders of a massive orgasm rumbling through her. And when he thrust his finger into her ass in time with his own orgasm, the sensation of being doubly-filled sent her tumbling over into a dark, wild void full of crackles of lightning and booms of thunder and an eternity of stars going supernova all around her.

Cliché, maybe, but he'd shattered her. No, she corrected herself as she sagged against him, *they'd shattered each other.*

For a while, they stayed motionless, her forehead resting against his until she had her breath back. Then she eased off of him and curled up beside him as his fingertips traced lazy patterns on her naked skin.

"I love you," he said, the words simple and direct, as if there had never been any doubt between them. As if they hadn't had to fight for what they now had.

"I know," she said, because it was true. And because the past was gone, and all that existed now was the two of them and the future.

"If I could fix this, I would."

There was a tightness in his voice, and she lifted her head, shifting her position just enough so that she could see his face. "There's nothing to fix, I promise. I had a bad day, but you've made it all better."

"It's not enough," he said, and she felt that twist in her gut. She hadn't meant to disturb him. To make him feel guilty about the house or the show.

"It is. I love this house. I love you. And, honestly, I even love the show. I'd just hit a wall, but you've helped me scale it."

"Maybe part way, but we're not over it yet." He cupped his chin, his mouth curved into a frown. Clearly, he was thinking, but she had no idea about what.

"Spencer?"

"They're the ones that crossed the line," he said. "The house is ours. This life is ours. And we're the couple on the show."

"So?"

"All that was agreed on. They got access. Not to our bedroom, God forbid." His eyes danced with amusement. "We're not *that* kind of a show. But they get to go pretty much everywhere else. They film our talks about groceries while we're discussing wallpaper. They film our talks about how we work and what kind of office space we need while we discuss furniture choices. Our lives seep into this show because they have to."

"I know all of that."

He took her hands in his. "But we've never staged anything."

She nodded slowly. "The party. That's why it's bugging me so much. It's not really our party at all."

"Would you have had an engagement party here?"

She shook her head. "We're already engaged. We went to The Fix and hung out with friends that night, remember?"

"I have a vague memory," he said, and she rolled her eyes.

"I say we take it away from them."

Her eyes went wide. "You mean tell them they can't film the party?"

"I mean cancel the party."

She lifted a shoulder. "Knowing Molly and Adam, they'd just reschedule."

"Can't have an engagement party if we're not engaged. And after we cancel, we can lay down the law. No more staged events."

He'd kept talking, but she barely heard anything after *not engaged.* How could she when the blood had rushed from her body, taking with it her brain's ability to function? "I—Spencer—what?"

She heard the horror and shock and confusion in her voice, but there was no other way for her to say those words.

For a moment, he stared at her, confused. Then his eyes went wide, and he said, "Oh, shit!" with such humor that she at least knew that nothing was wrong between them. But she still didn't know the punch line.

"What did you mean by 'not engaged'?"

He forced himself to stop chuckling, then drew in a breath. "It just occurred to me that the best way to render an engagement party moot is to not be engaged. And the only way I intend to not be engaged to you is when we're actually married."

"Oh."

"It's Friday, Angel. What do you say we fly to Vegas in the morning and get married? Then *we* can have a small reception at The Fix."

"You want to get married tomorrow?" Her head was spinning.

"I know it's not a fancy wedding, but we haven't even started planning since the show is taking so much time. But if you'd rather wait and have a big wedding, I certainly won't argue. I want you to have the wedding you want. I'd never try to—"

"*Yes*," she blurted.

"Yes?" His brows rose, as if he wasn't certain he'd heard her right.

"Yes," she repeated. Her heart was pounding, full of so much love she wasn't sure her body was capable of holding it all in. "Vegas sounds amazing. Because honestly, the only wedding I want is one where I end up married to you."

A slow smile crossed his mouth—joy, love, passion, friendship. It all mixed together in the soup that was their life. A life that had followed a crooked path, and would turn once more tomorrow when they went from being engaged to being married.

The thought overwhelmed her in the best of ways, and she rose up, needing nothing else in that moment except to kiss him, slow and deep.

The kind of kiss that sealed a promise—or a wedding vow.

OCTOBER

GAME DAY WINGS

REUBEN SLIDERS

CORN DIP FRITTERS

(CANDY CORN JELL-O SHOT)

NOVEMBER

COUNTRY FRIED STEAK BITES WITH GRAVY

SAUSAGE BISCUITS WITH BLACK & BLUE JAM

PUMPKIN PIE WITH CINNAMON WHIPPED TOPPING

(SPIKED APPLE CIDER)

DECEMBER

BUTTERNUT SQUASH SOUP

CRANBERRY TURKEY MELT

WHITE CHOCOLATE CRANBERRY COOKIES

(POINSETTIA)

SHORT STORY

JUST A KISS:
ERIC & TIFFANY

Game Day Wings

3 pounds chicken wings, cut into thirds and tips discarded

½ cup hot sauce

1 tablespoon Montreal steak seasoning

1 teaspoon salt

6 cups oil, for frying

8 tablespoons (1 stick) butter

1 bottle Russian dressing

In a large bowl, toss the wings with ¼ cup hot sauce, steak seasoning and salt. Cover and refrigerate for 30 minutes. Heat oil in a deep fryer or Dutch oven to 375 degrees. Fry wings in oil until crisp and a meat thermometer reads 165 degrees, about 10-12 minutes. Drain on paper towels. While the wings are draining, melt butter in a small bowl for 1 minute in the microwave. Add remaining ¼ cup hot sauce and Russian dressing to the butter and mix well. Transfer wings to a large bowl and pour sauce over them. Toss to coat and serve.

Reuben Sliders

12 slider potato buns

½ cup Thousand Island dressing

1 pound deli corned beef, shaved

½ pound thinly sliced Swiss cheese

½ cup sauerkraut

2 tablespoons butter, melted

1 teaspoon Worcestershire sauce

Preheat oven to 350 degrees. Slice potato buns in half and place bottom half in a 9x9-inch baking dish. Spread ¼ cup dressing over buns, then top with corned beef, Swiss cheese and sauerkraut. Spread remaining dressing on remaining bun halves and place on top of sauerkraut. Stir together melted butter and Worcestershire sauce and brush over the top of the buns. Cover with foil and bake for 15 minutes. Remove foil and bake for 5 minutes or until golden brown.

Corn Dip Fritters

6 ears grilled corn

8 ounces cream cheese

1 cup mayonnaise

1 cup Parmesan cheese

1 tablespoon garlic powder

¼ cup chopped green onion

½ cup chopped pickled jalapenos

1 teaspoon each salt and pepper

1 cup shredded cheddar cheese

For Fritters:

2 cups all-purpose flour

4 eggs

4 cups panko breadcrumbs

6 cups oil, for frying

This recipe is made with leftover Grilled Corn Dip.

GRILLED CORN DIP

Preheat oven to 350 degrees. Remove corn from the cob and mix together all ingredients except cheddar cheese. Place in a baking dish and top with cheddar cheese. Bake for 30 minutes.

Cool, then refrigerate overnight. Roll dip into 1-inch balls and coat with flour. Place on a cookie sheet and refrigerate for 30 minutes. Heat oil in a Dutch oven or deep fryer to 350 degrees. In a medium bowl, whisk 4 eggs. In a separate medium bowl, add the panko breadcrumbs. Remove the balls from the refrigerator and dredge each one in the egg then the panko breadcrumbs. Place 4 balls at a time in the oil and fry 1-2 minutes or until golden brown. Drain on paper towels.

Candy Corn Jell-O Shot

2 cups water

3 (7 grams each) envelopes unflavored gelatin

14 ounces sweetened condensed milk

1 cup Grey Goose vodka

1 box orange flavored Jell-O

Yellow food coloring

20 shot glasses

In a small saucepan, bring ½ cup water and 1 packet of unflavored gelatin to a simmer, until gelatin has dissolved. Remove from heat and add ½ can (7 ounces) of the sweetened condensed milk to the mixture. Stir until the ingredients combine. Add 1/3 cup vodka. Evenly distribute the first half of the mixture in the 20 shot glasses, but DO NOT fill more than 1/3 of the way full. Refrigerate the shots until firm, about 30-40 minutes. When the first layer is firm, pour another 1 cup of water into a saucepan and add 1 packet of gelatin to make the middle layer. Warm the water until the gelatin dissolves, remove from heat, and stir in the box of orange Jell-O until dissolved. Add 1/3 cup vanilla vodka. Evenly distribute orange layer on top of white layer and refrigerate until chilled. In a small saucepan, bring ½ cup water and 1 packet of gelatin to a simmer until gelatin has dissolved. Remove from the heat and add the remaining 7 ounces of sweetened condensed milk and a few drops of yellow food coloring. Distribute the yellow layer on top of the orange and put shot glasses back into the fridge until set.

Country Fried Steak Bites with Gravy

3 cups oil, for frying

2 eggs

2 cups milk

3 cups flour

Salt and Pepper

8-10 pieces cubed steak, cut into 3 strips each

Heat the oil in a Dutch oven or frying pan to 350 degrees. Mix together the eggs and milk. Salt and pepper the steak and add to the milk mixture. Place the flour in a 9x13-inch baking dish. Remove the meat and dredge in the flour. Fry about 4-6 pieces at a time, depending on size, for 3-5 minutes on each side. Remove from pan and allow to drain on paper towels. When all meat has been cooked, turn off heat and drain excess oil from the pan – leaving the pan drippings for the gravy.

MILK GRAVY

2 tablespoons flour

3 cups milk

½ tablespoon salt

1 tablespoon pepper

Pan drippings

Place the pan back on the burner and turn on low. Add 2 tablespoons flour and stir to get the drippings loose from the bottom of the pan. When the flour is incorporated with the drippings, add the milk, salt and pepper. Stir gravy continuously until it reaches a full boil. Remove from heat while continuing to stir until gravy has thickened to your preference.

Sausage Biscuits with Black & Blue Jam

8 tablespoons (1 stick) butter

4 cups biscuit mix (I use Bisquick)

1 cup sour cream

1 cup Sprite

1 cup ground sausage, cooked and drained

Preheat oven to 425 degrees. Melt butter in the microwave for 1 minute, then distribute evenly into 24 mini cupcake tins, just coating the bottom. Mix the biscuit mix, sour cream and Sprite together and knead dough for about 2 minutes. Mix in sausage until evenly distributed. Drop dough from a tablespoon into each mini cupcake tin, filling ¾ full. Bake for 15 minutes and serve with Black & Blue Jam.

BLACK & BLUE JAM

2 cups blueberries

2 cups blackberries

5 cups sugar

½ cup water

1 packet liquid pectin

6 jelly jars with lids

Puree the first 2 ingredients in a food processor or blender and place in a medium saucepan with the sugar and water. Bring to a boil over medium heat, stirring constantly. After the mixture has been boiling for 1 minute, add the pectin and continue to stir for 4 minutes. Turn off the heat and allow to thicken for an additional 4 minutes. Then ladle the mixture into the jelly jars, leaving 1/2 inch headspace. Apply caps and let jam stand in refrigerator until set, about 12 hours, or transfer to a pressure cooker to seal for a longer shelf life. If you are not using a pressure cooker to seal the jars, the jam must stay refrigerated. Refrigerated jams are good for about 3 months and sealed jars have a shelf life of about 18 months to two years.

Pumpkin Pie with Cinnamon Whipped Topping

1 (15 ounce) can pumpkin

1 (14 ounce) can sweetened condensed milk

2 eggs

1 teaspoon cinnamon

1 teaspoon nutmeg

1 frozen pie crust

Preheat oven to 425 degrees. Using a hand mixer, beat together pumpkin, sweetened condensed milk, eggs, cinnamon and nutmeg. Pour into pie crust and bake for 15 minutes. Reduce heat to 350 degrees and continue to bake for an additional 40 minutes. Top with Cinnamon Whipped Topping.

CINNAMON WHIPPED TOPPING

2 cups heavy cream

¼ cup sugar

1 teaspoon cinnamon

1 teaspoon vanilla extract

Using a stand mixer with the whisk attachment (or hand mixer), pour heavy cream in bowl and whisk on high, slowly adding the remaining ingredients until stiff peaks form.

Spiked Apple Cider

1 cup spiced apple cider

6 ounces Makers Mark bourbon

4 teaspoons maple syrup

Fill cocktail shaker with ingredients and 3-4 ice cubes. Shake and serve in a high ball glass with Mini Caramel Apples.

MINI CARAMEL APPLES

5 Granny Smith apples

1 container caramel dip

1 cup salted peanuts, chopped

melon ball scoop

40 toothpicks

Using a melon scoop, remove 8-10 balls from each apple, placing skin/flat side down on waxed paper. Place a toothpick in the top center of each apple ball. Microwave the caramel dip as instructed on the label. Dip each ball in the caramel and place on waxed paper. Spread the peanuts evenly on the top of each ball or leave plain. Place in the refrigerator for at least 10 minutes to set.

Butternut Squash Soup

1 butternut squash, peeled, seeded, and cut into 1-inch pieces

1 onion, diced

2 carrots, diced

2 tablespoons olive oil

1 tablespoon minced garlic

Salt and pepper to taste

3 cups chicken stock

4 slices bacon, cooked and crumbled

¼ cup freshly grated Parmesan cheese

Preheat oven to 400 degrees. Place squash, onion and carrots in a large bowl and coat with olive oil and garlic. Place in a single layer on a cookie sheet and season with salt and pepper. Bake for 30 minutes, or until squash is tender. Place roasted vegetables and chicken stock in a large pot. Bring to a boil, then reduce heat to simmer for 5-10 minutes or until slightly thickened. Using an immersion blender, puree vegetables until smooth. Serve with crumbled bacon and Parmesan cheese.

Cranberry Turkey Melt

8 slices Texas toast

4 tablespoons Dijon mustard

8 slices Muenster cheese

1 pound roasted turkey breast, sliced

8 tablespoons cranberry sauce

4 tablespoons mayonnaise

Heat a large skillet over medium heat. Spread 8 slices of bread with Dijon mustard and layer 4 slices with cheese, turkey, cranberry sauce and second slice of cheese. Top with remaining slices of bread, making 4 sandwiches. Spread outside of bread (both sides) with mayonnaise to coat evenly. Place sandwiches in skillet one or two at a time, pressing down firmly with the back of a spatula. Cook on each side for 2-3 minutes or until golden brown.

CRANBERRY SAUCE

4 cups fresh cranberries

1 cup sugar

½ cup orange juice

In a medium saucepan, combine all ingredients and simmer on low for 8-10 minutes, stirring and smashing until thickened. Refrigerate in an airtight container for at least 1 hour before use.

White Chocolate Cranberry Cookies

1 stick butter, softened

1 ½ cups sugar

1 egg

1 teaspoon vanilla extract

2 ¾ cups all-purpose flour

1 teaspoon baking soda

1 teaspoon baking powder

1 ½ cups white chocolate chips

1 cup dried cranberries

Preheat oven to 350 degrees. In a large bowl, using a hand mixer, cream together butter and sugar until smooth, then add egg and vanilla. Slowly add flour, baking soda and baking powder until blended. Stir in the white chocolate chips and cranberries. Place 1 tablespoon at a time on a greased cookie sheet. Bake for 12-14 minutes.

Poinsettia

1 cup fresh cranberries

1 bottle champagne

1 bottle cranberry juice

Place 2-3 cranberries in each ice cube compartment in an ice cube tray. Fill with water and freeze. To serve: In a high ball glass add 2-3 ice cubes and pour equal parts champagne and cranberry juice.

Short Story

JUST A KISS: ERIC & TIFFANY

Chapter One

"And that's my day," Tiffany Russell chirped, sliding easily under the bar so that she could put her tips into the jar that the servers, bartenders, and bar backs shared. That section of the bar swung open, but she'd gotten used to simply scooting under. Which was good, since customers tended to walk by and leave empty glasses on the supposed-to-stay empty section of the polished oak bar.

"I'm off as soon as Eric gets here, too," Cam said, easing down from where he'd just returned a bottle of top-shelf gin to its place.

She and Cameron Reed had worked together for years at The Fix on Sixth, which, as far as Tiffany was concerned was the best place to hang out and have a drink in the entire city of Austin. Maybe even all of Texas. They'd never dated, but they'd hit it off immediately and had become fast friends.

"I just put in an order for some Mushroom Spinach Risotto Balls and some Farmhouse Sliders for me and Mina. Wanna join?" He pointed to a table by the currently empty stage, where his girlfriend of almost a year, Mina, sat making notes on a script.

"Are you kidding? That would be great. I want to hear all about the new movie."

Tiffany and Mina had gone to high school together in Austin, and while Tiffany was still in school working toward her masters in psychology, Mina was working for a local indie film company that was doing exceptionally well.

"Plus, you're starving, right?"

Tiffany laughed. "Busted. You know me too well."

"I'm guessing your fridge is down to chunks of unidentifiable cheeses, a package of rice cakes—which are gross, by the way—and a flat Diet Coke."

Tiffany rolled her eyes. "Oh, please. I also have two limes and a carton of half-and-half."

"Went wild at the grocery store, I see."

"That's me. Always doing the crazy."

The front door opened, and Eric Shay stepped in off of Sixth Street. Immediately, Tiffany's eyes went to him. *Just like Pavlov's dog,* she thought, which was one of the downsides of being a pysch major. Too hard to hide from her own subconscious.

In this case, her id was definitely controlling the show. Her mouth was dry, her pulse had kicked up, and she was going to have to work very hard not to sound like a babbling idiot around him. All because she'd been living for almost a year now with the world's biggest crush on the dark-haired man with the action-hero body. A man who, apparently, was determined to spin her hormones into a tizzy, because in addition to the jeans that clung to his muscled thighs, he also wore a tank top that clung to his chest and revealed every inch of his tight-but-not-too-bulky arms.

It was, frankly, seriously distracting.

Even in mid-March he was tan, and he looked like a god. Or at least like a fitness model. Which was probably a more reasonable comparison, considering his tank top advertised the Capital 10K, a local Austin marathon that Tiffany knew he'd participated in for each of the last six years. And, she assumed, he'd be running in his seventh in just a few weeks.

So would she, actually.

She'd started running with Mina and two other women who used to work at The Fix. Megan, who'd married Parker Manning after a whirlwind relationship and was about to launch a skin care line. And Taylor, who used to stage manage the Man of the Month calendar contest, but was now happily engaged to one of the winners and working with Spencer and Brooke on *Mansion Makeover,* their real estate reality show.

"You're starting to drool," Cam whispered to her, and she actually rubbed her mouth before realizing he was teasing her. She grabbed a bar rag and smacked him, only to realize that Eric had come even closer and had seen the whole weird interplay.

She waved lamely, feeling not sexy and interesting, but like a twelve-year-old wrestling with her BFF. Way to make a good impression.

Eric waved back, then told Cam he'd be out to relieve him as soon as he changed into the bar's black logo T-shirt.

"No problem," Cam said, then turned back to Tiffany. If he was trying to hold in laughter, he wasn't doing a good job of it.

At least no one was sitting along the bar at the moment. Four o'clock on a Sunday was the bar's slowest time, and most people who came in sat at a table and ordered food. And none of the folks at any of the tables seemed to be paying any attention to her and Cam. Except Mina, who quickly turned back to her script, her expression amused, when Tiffany caught her eye.

"You need to just go for it," Cam said.

"Hello? I'd planned to last year, remember?"

"How could I forget? You spent days stressing about whether the whole Ben thing made it weird."

She lifted a shoulder. "I know, but I'm over it now."

Her original excuse for not pursuing anything with Eric had been that she'd dated his brother Ben for six months when she was an undergrad. He was six years older than Tiffany and at the time he'd been a teaching assistant in the psych department. It wasn't a grand passion, but they'd had great conversations. It had ended when he entered a doctoral program at a college in the Northeast—where he now had a teaching position—and Tiffany had only realized how uninspired the relationship had been when his leaving hadn't left a hole in her heart. He was a nice guy, just not *her* guy.

Her guy would make her tingle. Her guy would generate sparks. He'd make her laugh. He'd make her *feel.*

Ben simply wasn't that guy.

But she thought that Eric might be…

"If you're over it, then why haven't you done anything?" Cam asked reasonably.

"Because right about the time I got over it, he started going out with that girl."

"That was last September. And they broke up before Christmas. And now it's March. Look at all the weeks you've wasted."

She made a face. "Well, if I'd made a move earlier, then I would have been the rebound girl."

"Procrastination, much?"

"Dammit, Cam. Have you thought that maybe he just doesn't like me?"

"Or maybe he's the one who thinks it's too weird to ask you out."

"I don't know. I only saw him a couple of times when Ben and I were together. I felt guilty for thinking he was hot—and kept my mouth shut, of course—but I don't think he noticed me at all."

Cam shrugged. "Maybe he didn't. Then again, maybe you were wrong."

"And maybe he's not even remotely interested now."

"Dunno. But the point is neither do you until you do something about it." His expression shifted to one of sympathy. "Come on, Tiff. You're the one who helped me finally get Mina, remember? I want to do the same to you."

"I know. Thanks. I'm just chicken."

"Yeah, well, you know what they say."

"What?"

He leaned toward her. "Get over it."

She rolled her eyes and was tempted to hit him with the bar rag again, but Eric was on his way back.

Cam was scooting under the bar, and she was about to follow. "Hold up. Why don't you make us a pitcher of Pinot Punch? Appetizers should be out soon."

"I can do that," Eric said as he passed Cam, then ducked under the bar and emerged about two feet from Tiffany. She was a full head shorter, and she tilted her head up to smile at him.

"Love the hair," he said as Cam headed off toward Mina.

"Oh." She reached up and pushed an errant curl off her face. Her friend Selma had referred Tiff to her hairdresser, and now her wavy light brown hair was highlighted with streaks of magenta. "Thanks. And I can get the drink. You have opening stuff to do."

"You sure?"

When she nodded, he gave her a thumbs-up then started to pass by her to get to the prep station. But there was a box of wine in the narrow walk space, and since she hadn't anticipated his movement, she couldn't get completely clear of him. He ended up passing her sideways, so that for one moment they were facing each other and the air between them crackled, sparking with possibility.

His chocolate brown eyes met hers, and she thought she saw a desire as potent as her own.

Then he was past her and the earth started turning again—and the moment evaporated, and she was left to wonder if she'd really seen it, or if it had all been her imagination.

She stayed there like an idiot until she heard him call from the end of the bar, "We moved the pitchers over there."

"Oh." She followed his gaze to the location of the pitchers, which she already knew, then called back her thanks. Then she went about pulling the ingredients for what was one of her favorite drinks served at The Fix. She was concentrating on measuring out the orange juice when Eric came up behind her and put his hand on her shoulder.

She squeaked, dropped the OJ carton, and spun around.

"Oh, shit," she said, glancing between him and the rapidly spreading pool of juice. "I'm so sorry."

"I didn't mean to startle you. Just the opposite. I was going to pass behind you, so I was giving you a silent warning. Sorry."

"It's okay. Really." She dove beneath the counter for a box of rags and started to mop up the mess.

"Go on," he said. "I'll make the drink and bring it to you."

"I can't ask you to—"

"You're not." This time, she was expecting it when he reached out and lightly put his hand on her upper arm as if to steady her. A place that she was now hyper aware of. "I'm offering," he said, and once again she saw that heat in his eyes

"I—oh. If you're sure?"

"Just pop your head in the back and tell Mike I need him," he added, referring to the part-time bar back.

"Sure. Thanks." They were close now, and suddenly she had the completely unreasonable impression that he was going to kiss her. Which couldn't possibly be true, but she eased out of his grip, anyway.

He stood up straighter, and she slipped under the bar. "Thanks again," she said, then hurried to sit with Mina and Cam, taking a seat with her back to the bar so she wouldn't be tempted to stare.

"What was that all about?" Cam asked.

"I'll never manage to ask him out. I'm acting like a teenager with a crush. When it's perfectly obvious that I'm a twenty-four-year-old with a crush. It's absurd. I'm absurd."

"Wait," Mina said. The food had been delivered, and she used the slider she held in one hand as a pointer. "You have a crush on Eric?"

Tiffany turned her attention to Cam. "You didn't tell her?"

Cam's shoulders rose. "You told me not to."

Tiffany and Mina exchanged glances, then both started laughing.

"What?" Cam asked.

Mina shook her head, then took his hand. "You're a really good guy. You know that, right?"

"I just thought—"

"Maybe a movie?" Mina said, her voice pitched a bit too loud.

He's there? Tiffany mouthed to Cam, who lifted his brows in acknowledgment and sipped his water.

Tiffany's pulse, which had calmed down, kicked up again.

"Looks good," Eric said, eyeing the food as he put the pitcher of Pinot Punch—a mix of pinot grigio, orange juice, peach schnapps, frozen peach slices, and Sprite—on the table.

"Thanks for doing that," Tiffany said. "And sorry again for being such a klutz."

"Yeah, well, at least you're a pretty klutz." He held her eyes for a heartbeat, then looked away, almost as if he'd startled himself with his own bravado.

As if sensing the need for intervention, Mina asked Eric what he was doing later. Spring Break officially started the next day. "You don't usually have a day off after a shift, do you?"

"Nope," Eric said. "But I also usually work until closing. I'm only on the clock for five hours tonight. Off at nine. Reece said he'd come in and cover for me."

"Hot date?" Cam asked, and Tiffany kicked him under the table.

"Not exactly. Pretty much everyone in my apartment complex either goes to UT or recently graduated. So there's a party tonight in the courtyard. When I mentioned it to Reece, he offered to cover for me. To be honest, I wasn't planning on going, but when your boss tells you to go to a party…" He trailed off with a shrug.

"Sounds like fun," Mina said. "Why weren't you going to go?"

He shrugged, his eyes cutting quickly to Tiffany and then back to Mina. "I've only lived in this apartment for a few months, so I don't know many of them yet. Guess I wasn't in the mood to go stag."

"So take someone," Cam said.

"Sure," Mina added. "Why don't you take Tiffany?"

"What?" Tiffany said.

"Yeah?" Eric shifted to look at her. "I'd love the company if you're up for it."

"I—" She looked helplessly at Cam and Mina, both of whom were urging her on with their eyes. "Well, yeah. That sounds fun."

Eric's wide smile lit up her heart. "All right, then," he said. "It's a date."

"Yeah," Tiffany repeated, her voice raised above the cacophony of hooting and hollering going on in her head. "A date."

Chapter Two

A few hours ago, Eric wanted to kiss Mina almost as much as Tiffany. Now, as he sipped a beer in his kitchen while he waited for Tiffany to arrive, he was thinking that he should have muzzled her. Because right now, his nerves were definitely jumping.

That was the thing about Tiffany—somehow, someway, she always knocked him off balance.

As a general rule, Eric didn't get nervous around women. Considering how much his tips improved when he flirted, a case of nerves would be pretty inconvenient. And even when there was a real attraction, he'd never felt as topsy-turvy as he did around Tiffany.

Jill, for example. They'd met in the produce section of HEB last September, flirted casually, and Jill had asked if he wanted to meet for coffee. One thing had led to another, and before he knew it, they were dating.

There'd been sparks—in bed at least—and that's probably why he let it go on so long. But even with sparks there wasn't any real heat. And every time she'd left him to go home or to work, she tended to leave his thoughts as well.

Tiffany hadn't left his thoughts—not really—for years. She always seemed to linger. That crooked smile. Her hair that fell in such lovely waves he imagined it felt like silk under his fingers. And those greenish-gray eyes the color of the sky after a thunderstorm.

He shouldn't want her; Eric knew that. It seemed disloyal to be attracted to his brother's ex-girlfriend, even if Ben was half a continent away. Eric knew how much Ben had loved her, though Ben had never used the word. Even so, Eric had been able to see it in his older brother's eyes.

Could Eric date someone his brother had loved? What if it got serious? For that matter, what if he somehow ended up hurting her? Would it end up being an issue between him and his brother as well as him and Tiffany?

"Idiot," he said, and slammed the beer bottle into his trashcan. He was seriously overthinking this. He had yet to go on a date with her, and already he was planning how to handle their possible futures, both good and bad? Honestly, he should get his head examined.

A small laugh escaped him. Maybe he should get Tiffany to do that for him. She was a psych major, after all. And if she wanted to continue the inspection more intimately… well, that would be fine by him.

He grabbed another beer from his fridge and told himself to chill. This wasn't a date; they were just going to a party together. Friends and coworkers. So there was nothing disloyal going on. And there was no reason to be nervous.

Right? *Right.*

He checked the clock, saw that she was ten minutes late, and wondered if she was blowing him off.

Three minutes later, he heard her knock, and he hurried to the door, knowing that he was going to come off as over-eager, but not really caring. All he wanted was to see her, and when he pulled open the door, she took his breath away.

She stood in front of him with her hair flowing loose around her face, her lips a soft, kissable pink. She wore a pale blue T-shirt dress that hit mid-thigh and blue sandals. Her toenails were blue, too, and so perfect that he fleetingly wondered if she'd had a pedicure before coming over. And if so, he wondered if it was for him.

"You look great," he said, meaning it. His cousin Sarah wore that kind of dress all the time, but they hung shapeless and uninteresting on her. With Tiffany, there was nothing dull or shapeless about the outfit. She gave it curves. Made it unique. Hell, it was practically runway ready the way she wore it.

A slow smile spread across her face, lighting her eyes with pleasure. "I'm glad you think so." She stepped inside, and he caught the scent of vanilla. It made him hungry, although not for food.

"It's a little summery," she was saying, and he forced his mind away from how good she smelled. "But the weather's so crazy lately that I think March is turning into summer."

"That's okay," he said. "That would mean December would come, when? In September? Three months early. I can handle that."

"Hmm. Good point. But does that mean that May's already behind us? Because that means I didn't get everything in this semester. I don't want to crash and burn in my masters program just because I wore a dress out of season."

"Right. So that's no good. How about we let the months stay the same, and we'll just call the dress a Tiffany Russell fashion statement."

"That's me. The ultimate trendsetter." She looked around. "Nice apartment."

"If by nice you mean completely uninteresting, then I agree with you."

She laughed. "Well, it is a little sparse. But it has potential."

She was right on both counts.

"The potential's why I rented it," he said. "I like the open floor plan so I can get in and out of the kitchen easily. The master bedroom is huge, and there's a smaller bedroom for guests."

"Have a lot of those?"

"Not really, but my cousin's a single mom. Sometimes I watch her little boy. When she needs some sanity time. Or when she needs sex and wants him out of the house."

Tiffany burst out laughing. "Lucky she has you. That explains the two-bedroom. I'm guessing the big kitchen is so you can fiddle around with drink mixes and appetizers?"

"You got it." For years, he'd been experimenting with making cocktails, and Tyree had even put a few of his creations on the menu at The Fix. But it was only since The Fix sponsored a food fair last October that he'd started trying a hand in the kitchen. He wasn't great—not yet—but he enjoyed it. And he wanted to speak the language of food as well as he did that of alcohol. To be able to pair things without a recipe book, but simply because he knew the essence of the ingredients.

"That explains the layout," she said. "But you have a card table to eat on, a futon for a couch, a bookshelf that's overflowing—some awesome titles, by the way—some milk crates supporting a piece of plywood for a coffee table. What's in the bedroom? A blow-up air mattress?"

"Want me to show you?" The instant he spoke, he regretted it. The words might be innocent, but his intention definitely wasn't. From the way she tilted her head to the side, he was certain she'd heard the underlying invitation. When her cheeks flushed and she flashed a tiny half-smile before saying, "Maybe later," he was sure of it. And the fact that he'd heard as much heat as humor in that response not only gave him cause to be optimistic, it also gave him a hard-on.

"Right." He cleared his throat, then turned toward the kitchen, both so that he could offer her a drink and so that he could hide some of the evidence that she was making him crazy.

Despite the open floor plan, there was still a small breakfast bar off the counter near the refrigerator, and he gestured for her to sit there.

"Want a drink before we go down?"

"Down?"

"The party's in the pool building. There's a bar down there, but I can't vouch for the offerings."

Eric was a drink snob, a fact that pretty much everyone at the bar knew. Not that he didn't think there was a place for cheap alcohol, but he'd decided long ago to make his living tending bar until he could move up to owning his own place. Before that, he'd considered being a sommelier—his palate was excellent—but had quickly learned that he liked the social aspect of tending bar. His parents had been less than enthusiastic when he'd told them, but when he paid his own way through business school at UT so that he'd have the skills to open a restaurant when the time came, they got on board.

Plus, they really appreciated having someone in the family who could make a decent margarita.

Which, frankly, seemed like a good idea now.

When he suggested it, Tiffany nodded enthusiastically. "Much better than the cheap wine and beer they have downstairs, I'm sure. Besides, I'm in no hurry if you aren't."

He met her eyes. "No hurry at all."

Two margaritas each later, and they still weren't in a hurry. They had, however, moved to the futon. Or Eric had. Tiffany was sitting the floor on the other side of the table, her legs straight out in front of her, her hands behind her to prop herself up. Every few minutes, she'd lean forward and take a sip of her drink, a process that caused her dress to shift and cling in a way that made Eric glad he was seated.

Almost an hour had passed, and they were talking about everything and nothing. Currently, about Tiffany's plan to run in the Capital 10K. "Since when are you a runner?"

"I'm a runner," she said indignantly. "I'm just not an experienced runner. But I'm getting better."

"Didn't we have a conversation about this time last year when you told me I was—how did you put it—battier than the bats under the bridge if I thought that running ten kilometers in the Texas heat sounded like a good time?"

"No contradiction at all," she said. "I'm obviously just as crazy as you are."

"Come here."

One eyebrow rose. "Why?"

"Come. Here."

She narrowed her eyes, but she stood, a little bit wobbly, and not in an Emily Post approved manner, either. But he didn't complain—even if the quick flash of her pale blue panties almost sent him over the edge.

He casually grabbed a pillow and put it on his lap, then pointed in front of him. She moved to stand there, but eyed him dubiously.

"What?"

He didn't answer. Just reached out and cupped his hand around her leg, just above the knee. Slowly, he slid his hand up, stroking her thigh, feeling the firm, taut muscles. Feeling her tremble.

"You're right," he said, his voice low. "Definitely a runner's leg."

She exhaled, a low, soft sound that curled inside of him. He wanted to hear more. He wanted to know all the little noises she made. And she wasn't stopping him. He could keep moving up and up and up, and dear God he was so tempted to touch every inch of her and—

A sharp knock at the door made them both jump, and she scrambled that way, not looking at him.

"Who is it?"

"Party patrol!"

She looked over her shoulder and tossed him a grin. He wondered if her thoughts tracked his—he was thinking that the patroller had just killed one potential party.

She opened the door. A neighbor he recognized—John? Maybe Jake?—stood there with an empty Lone Star beer bottle.

"Dude, you're missing out. We're about to play spin the bottle. We're totally going retro."

"Sounds great," Eric said. "We'll be down soon."

"Will we?" she asked, closing the door, and while her words sent shockwaves of anticipation scurrying through him like electrons, he wasn't sure if he was hearing what he thought he was hearing.

She came back, this time sitting on the couch beside him, so close he caught the scent of vanilla. "I'm surprised it's spin the bottle," she said. "I thought Never Have I Ever was all the rage now."

"I've been out of school for a couple of years now. Despite the west campus address, I'm pretty out of touch with those wacky kids today."

"But you know the game, right? You ask a question. And if you *have* done it, you drink. And in the version my friends and I've played, if you *haven't* done it, you have to eradicate that omission if at all possible, right then and there."

"Give me a for example."

"Never have I ever eaten ice cream," she said. "I have, so I drink." She finished off her margarita. "And then I'd have to eat ice cream. But don't make me," she added. "It wouldn't mix with the margie."

"You're in luck, because I don't have any. But you're also out of your drink."

She tilted her head. "Does that mean you want to play?"

"Why not?"

"Cool." She got up and went to the kitchen, then came back with the blender, with enough still in it for each of them to have a fresh glass. Then she sat down next to him on the couch, her glass in hand. "Okay, you go first."

"All right. Never have I ever kissed a girl." He took a long sip of his margarita and kept his eyes on her, amused at the way her brows rose.

"Diving right into the good stuff, huh? Or are you just trying to work up a good bedtime fantasy?"

He was still swallowing, and he almost choked on the last comment, but she just batted her eyes and looked innocent. Then she took a drink.

"Who?" he said.

"Marjorie Frederick. Fourth grade. We were practicing." She shrugged. "Sorry. Nothing very fantasy-like there."

"Damn, and I really hoped."

"Did you?"

He shook his head. "Not that I'd object. But that's not my fantasy of you."

Damn, but he was getting bolder. Maybe making the margaritas extra strong wasn't such a great idea after all. Then again, considering the heated way she was looking at him now, maybe it was his most brilliant move ever.

"Your turn."

She nodded, a pink flush staining her neck and cheeks. "Never have I ever had a secret crush." She drank. And so did he.

"Me again," he said, and decided it was now or never. He lifted his glass. "Never have I ever kissed my secret crush." And then he very firmly put it down without taking a sip.

A heartbeat passed. Then another. Then she set her glass down.

"So." He swallowed. "You said we're supposed to fix that if possible. Can you?"

For a second, she didn't answer. Then she nodded. "What about you?"

"Me, too."

"Oh." She licked her lips, and in that moment the only thing he wanted to do was suck on that plump, sweet lower lip. "Tiffany," he said, "I'm going to kiss you now."

A wide smile illuminated her face. "Not if I kiss you first."

Chapter Three

Tiffany had imagined this moment for over a year. The feel of his mouth on hers, the strength of his hand cupping her neck. The heat that curled through her blood, rushing to her lips, her breasts, her sex.

In her imagination, she'd felt every touch, every breath, every gentle stroke, every hard demand. She'd roamed her body with her own hands, and she'd arched up, crying out in wild abandon when the man in her fantasy had made her come.

The Eric in her dreams had taken her to soaring heights, reducing her to nothing but limp, satisfied ashes.

But that Eric had nothing on the man now touching her, his lips hard and demanding. His hands possessive and strong. She wanted to melt into him, to lay herself out as an offering and let him feast on her. On all of her.

His hand moved, coming to cup her face. He held her in place, taking the kiss the way he wanted. His tongue tasting all of her. His teeth clashing with hers. Drawing blood and heat and working them both into a wild frenzy that only got more desperate when his hand moved down to cup her breast roughly, then lower still to thigh. She spread her legs, and—finally—he slid his hand all the way up her leg until he reached her core and her blue panties that were surely now dark, wet from her own desire. Dripping with need.

He slid his finger along the band of her panties, teasing her by occasionally slipping beneath the material, his tongue thrusting deeper when he did so. And then, damn or bless him, he thrust his finger deep inside her, his tongue mimicking the thrusting motion of his finger until her mind was spinning and her body burning and she finally couldn't take it anymore. This onslaught. This wicked, wonderful assault on her senses.

"Stop," she finally said, impressed that he did so immediately, though the expression on his face was so confused and frustrated she almost wanted to laugh. Instead, she drew her breath in, calming herself as she put her finger to his lip. "I need something."

Again, confusion darkened his eyes. "Anything."

She stood up, then very slowly pulled the dress up over her head. For a moment, she couldn't see his face, but when her head popped free of the material she saw an expression of such pure desire it seemed like worship.

She thought she should be embarrassed, standing there in nothing but her bra and panties, but she wasn't. On the contrary, she saw the desire reflected in her eyes, and she felt powerful. Like a sensual creature that he'd come to worship.

Except it wasn't worship she was looking for. She didn't want a sweet encounter. She wanted wild. Rough, even.

She wanted him to claim her. To make her his.

And she wanted it now.

Slowly, she stepped toward him. She'd long ago kicked off her sandals, and her body was so hyper-aware that it seemed as if she could feel every fiber of carpet beneath her feet. When she reached him, she held out her hand, and he stood. "I'm a little bit drunk, but I just want you to know that's not why I'm sleeping with you."

"No?" He had one hand on her waist, and the other was stroking her bare shoulder. Warmth flowed through her, originating with the sparks that the contact was generating and making it very hard to think.

She shook her head. "I've wanted this—you—for about forever. And thank goodness for liquid courage, because it's clearly doing the talking here. God knows I've been tongue-tied for months."

"Thank goodness is right," he said. "Because I've wanted you, too, and never worked up the nerve to do anything about it." He grinned. "Here's to my fabulous margaritas."

"Cheers to that." She bit her lower lip as the hand on her waist trailed up, and then made a small noise in her throat when both hands slipped behind her back to unfasten her bra, and then to gently tug it off.

"So beautiful."

She wasn't very big, barely a b-cup, but he didn't seem to mind. His look told her that as far as he was concerned, she was perfect. And that made her bold. "Sit back down. Watch me."

He did, and she put one bare foot on the couch between his legs, then touched her own breasts, watching the way his cock got hard under his jeans as she teased her nipples. Then how his hand moved to his fly when she slid one palm down slowly, lower and lower until her fingers grazed her panty line.

Their eyes were locked now, though she could see him stroking himself through his jeans, and oh, God, the sense of power, knowing that she was turning him on like that. She'd never done anything like this before. Sex was nice, but straightforward. With Eric she wanted twists and turns. She wanted to play. To explore.

She wanted, she realized, to have fun.

He lifted a brow, and she understood the question. She inclined her head just slightly, and he finished unzipping and took out his cock. She honestly wasn't an expert, but as far as she was concerned it was perfect. Thick and hard and looking as eager for her as she was to feel it inside her.

"Yes," she murmured, sliding her hand down to cup herself. She was so wet, and she thrust her two fingers inside, imagining it was Eric filling her. Eric telling her how good she felt, how tight she was.

"Please," she whispered. "I want it to be you."

"Take off your panties," he ordered, and she did, then walked naked in front of him. "Ride me," he said, taking her hand with her still slick fingers. And as she straddled him, still fully clothed—and oh, God, how hot was that?—he sucked her slick fingers as she rose and fell in a slow rhythm on his cock. A rhythm that got faster as she got closer—as she felt the tug of the rising orgasm rushing from his mouth on her fingers all the way down to her core.

"Yes," she cried, feeling her walls clench tight around his cock. "Eric, oh, please, oh, please."

But the plea died on her lips when his hands moved to her hips and stilled her. "Not just yet, baby," he said. And in one incredible motion, he stood up, one hand on her ass and the other on her back. And then, praise be, he carried her to the bedroom.

She was incredible.

That was all he could think. That she was incredible and that through some miracle, she was his. His to touch. To explore. To take.

And, oh, yes, he was going to take everything she gave, and more. He craved the feel of her, hungered to feel her tremble beneath him.

He wanted to take her right to the edge, leave her balanced there, and then, in one hard and final moment of bliss, to take her over and make them both break apart together.

That's what he wanted. But he wanted it slowly. And once he'd laid her out naked on the bed, he started at her ankle, then kissed his way up that beautiful calf to her runner's thigh, higher and higher along the soft skin of her inner thigh that twitched and jumped beneath his lips, fighting the sweet punishment he was administering.

He gave her just a hint, licking the soft area between her thigh and pussy before he teased her higher up, his tongue playing with her navel, his mouth sucking her breast, his lips brushing lightly over his collar bone. And through all of it, his cock was throbbing, rubbing the bedspread, then her legs, then her sweet, wet pussy.

"Pull your knees up," he ordered. "But keep them spread. And baby? I want you to look at me."

She did as he said, and he almost lost it just looking at her, wide and open and so ready for him. Then he rose over her, his hands on either side of her head as the tip of his cock teased her core and she made little whimpering sounds of need.

He bent forward and kissed her, wanting to taste those sounds, and she claimed his mouth so hungrily that the kiss deepened even as he thrust inside her. And then he couldn't stop. No power on earth could have made him stop. She was his, and this was their moment, and he thrust into her again and again, deeper, and then deeper still when she released one knee so that she could press her hand against the headboard.

She held her body steady as he ravaged her, going so deep they felt like one person. Until he was certain they were one person, because when he felt her start to go over, the contractions inside her milked his cock until he followed her out into space, lost and exhausted and feeling absolutely, deliciously wonderful.

He had no idea how long he lay like a man destroyed before reason returned. Then he stretched out beside her, their bodies touching, sharing her heat and feeling her heartbeat pound through him.

"That was so much better than my fantasies," she murmured.

"You have fantasies of me?"

She rolled over to face him. "Are you saying you didn't have any of me?"

"Hardly. I have a whole collection, all organized in my head according to theme."

She propped herself up on one elbow, the seductive well-fucked glow now mixing with the expression of an eager kitten. "Tell me."

"Too many to go through," he teased.

"A random sampling then."

"G, PG, R, or NC-17?"

"You have G-rated fantasies?"

"Ah, those are some of the best. A lazy afternoon in a boat or by the lake. Of course, that one can turn PG—or R—if it's set at Hippie Hollow," he added, referring to Austin's nude beach on Lake Travis.

"Only up to R?"

"No sex in the park. Otherwise..." He waggled his eyebrows and she laughed. "But other than shifts from G to Not-G, I think my favorite G-rated fantasy is making dinner with you—just experimenting, you know? And then sharing a bottle of wine in front of the television, your head in my lap and my finger stroking your hair."

"Sounds nice. What movie?"

"*Casablanca*."

"Oh, but she leaves. We need one where they're together at the end."

"I'll speak to the producers."

She nodded, as if that settled that. "And what about after? Does it stay G?"

"Oh, no. It moves on to NC-17. But we don't want to lose our rating. So that," he said with a quick kiss to her nose, "is the sequel."

"I like."

"And your fantasies?"

"A lot like this," she said. "And sometimes there are toys involved."

His cock stiffened at the thought, his mind going through all sorts of possibilities. "I do like the way your mind works."

She laughed, and he wondered how he got so lucky to have this woman in his life, especially when—

He closed his eyes, wishing his head hadn't started going in that direction.

"Eric?"

"Sorry. Mind wandering."

"Yeah?" She brushed his jawline with her fingertips. "Where to?"

"It's just— I mean— Oh, hell. Do you think we should talk about before? About you and Ben?"

She tugged her hand away. "Um, now? Because he's a great guy and all, but I really don't want him in bed with us. Do you?"

"I only—"

But her hand had slid down, and now she'd captured his cock. She stroked him, the movements firm and even and so goddamn erotic. Then she started to move down the bed, her body disappearing under the sheet. And before her head disappeared, she met his eyes and said once more. "Do you?"

And the only answer he had was—*No.*

Chapter Four

"You're really not going to tell me where we're going?" Tiffany asked.

"Nope. Because then you might chicken out."

She glanced into the back seat of his Jeep. "What's in the duffel?"

"Not telling."

She leaned back in her seat and huffed. "Beware how far you push me. You can withhold information, but I can withhold sex."

"A good point." They were heading south on Lamar from his place, and as soon as he crossed the river he turned right into the Zachary Scott Theater parking lot. "You've convinced me." He nodded at the duffel. "But if you peek, you'll ruin the surprise."

"I can live with that," she said, then lunged for the duffel, only to freeze with her hand on the zipper. After a moment, she plunked herself back into the seat, crossed her arms, and pretended to sulk. "It just better be good."

He laughed, something they'd been doing a lot of. They'd spent all day Monday in bed, with the exception of a quick jaunt outside when they sat outside by the pool reading and drinking cocktails. It seemed a good way to spend the first day of Spring Break, after all. Even if she was the only one still in school.

The only downside had been that the pool hadn't been cleaned for the season, and so they didn't actually swim. Which really was too bad, as the weather was unseasonably warm and the day had been as good as it gets. Or, it had seemed so until today, which started out fabulous and was fast approaching amazing.

They'd slept until nine, and then Tiffany had checked the weather. As soon as she'd seen the forecast, she'd made the calls—begging Lisa, a new server, to take her shift, and then calling Cam and telling him that she was in Eric's bed, and since this was partly his doing, he owed her. Which meant that he needed to cover Eric's shift that night.

She'd just ended the call when Eric opened his eyes and peered at her. "What did you do?"

"Wrangled us another day," she'd said. "You're welcome."

And now here they were, tooling through Austin with the top off his Jeep, and she was feeling as free and happy as she could remember feeling in a long, long time.

"This is one of the areas where I thought I might want to have my own bar someday," he said later as they were back on the road. They'd turned right onto Barton Springs Road and were passing the collection of restaurants, bars, and coffee shops that lined the road between Lamar Boulevard and Zilker Park.

"It's a good area," she said. "But a lot of competition. I don't know exactly what you're thinking of, but I see you as more of a neighborhood bar guy. A place where you know pretty much everyone who comes in."

The smile he flashed her was brilliant. "You read my mind. Because that's exactly why I talked myself out of this location. I'm thinking something in East Austin. A lot of revitalization going on over there."

"I think that's perfect."

"Just a plan right now," he said. "I need to make sure I have the chops first." He glanced sideways at her before making a turn into the park and heading toward the pool and the hillside theater area. "Can you keep a secret?"

"I managed not to tell anyone except Cam that I had a crush on you for ages. So I guess so."

"The Fix is doing so well after the contest and all the other promo that Tyree and the others are looking into opening a location off of South Congress. Kind of near where Derek and Amanda are renovating that old motel into a retro chic place to stay."

"Really? I hadn't heard."

"They asked if I wanted to manage it."

She leaped across the seat and hugged him. Fortunately, he'd already parked. "That's amazing. Eric, you'll do great! I'm so excited for you. And jealous. I still have years of school to go."

"Well, you can spend them in my bar studying."

She tilted her head, eyeing him. She knew he was just talking, but still…

"I'll take that offer, you know," she said softly, her chest tightening as she realized what she'd just said—not to mention how fast she'd said it compared to when they got together. But with Eric it felt right. Hell, it had felt right from the moment she'd first met him.

Whether or not it felt right to him, though…

He still hadn't answered, but he was looking at her with such an expression of trust and wonder that she couldn't help but hope that maybe, just maybe…

"Do you mean that?"

She nodded, her throat too thick to speak.

"Good. Because it's a standing offer."

Her whole body relaxed. "We took way too long getting here, you know."

"Zilker?" he joked, then immediately shook his head. "No, forget I said that. You're right. Way too long." He leaned over and kissed her, a sweet kiss, but with a promise of spice later. Even so, when they pulled apart, she thought she saw a shadow in his eyes. More, she thought she knew what it was about—they still hadn't talked about Ben.

And she didn't want to start now.

She cleared her throat. "So why are we here?"

"Get out, and I'll show you."

A few minutes later, they were standing at the gate to Barton Springs Pool. "You game?"

"Are you insane?" she countered. "I love this place but it's fricking cold."

"It's pure Austin and it's amazing. And if you stay close to me, I'll warm you up. Besides, Robert Redford learned to swim here, according to Wikipedia, anyway. Doesn't every woman want to be close to Redford?"

She rolled her eyes, but she couldn't argue. Maybe there was some Redford magic in the water.

A huge dammed-off section of Barton Creek, the pool was fed by an underground spring, which kept it at more or less sixty-eight degrees except in the hottest part of summer. Now, this early in spring, it was going to be chilly.

Still, she loved the pool and had spent much of her childhood there. Some of her happiest memories were of hanging out with her friends on floats on the water or blankets on the grass. And she had to admit she was eager to gather more happy memories with Eric.

Twenty minutes later, when she'd changed into the bathing suit he'd brought for her and was standing in the water turning blue, she was starting to think differently.

"You're going about it all wrong."

"If you say jump in, I'll splash you."

"Jump in," he said, and she splashed as promised. But all that did was have him stalk to her, and since she didn't want to slip on the rocks that formed the base of the shallow end, she couldn't scurry. Soon, he'd not only caught her in a kiss, he'd pulled her down onto the rocks, his body beneath hers, his mouth exploring hers.

She had no idea how he managed it, but during the length of that slow, heated kiss, he'd scooted them both further into the water. So that when they broke, she was halfway submerged, and still in his arms. "Another?" he asked, pulling her close. "They say body heat is the best way to stay warm."

"In that case," she said as she pressed hard against him, "you're going to be warming me all day."

Since Tiffany had a major paper to write over the break, she'd reluctantly gone home after their date, which had ended at Matt's El Rancho, where they'd devoured a dinner of cheese enchiladas and enough chips and hot sauce to fully warm them back up.

Now alone, she took a hot shower. Not because she was chilled, but because there was something sensual about the hot water sluicing over her as she thought of the way Eric touched her, and—

The ring of her phone cut off her thoughts, and she frowned, irritated at the aborted fantasy, but also grateful. Go down that road and she'd get no work done.

By the time she got out of the shower, the call had rolled to voicemail. Since she didn't recognize the number, she didn't bother listening straight away. Instead, she put on her most comfy sweats and T-shirt, then settled down at her kitchen table with her books and laptop spread around her.

She was just settling in to read an article from the *British Journal of Clinical Psychology,* when the phone rang again. Same number. She grabbed it up, expecting it was a robocall, but figuring she could block it if it was.

It wasn't.

It was Ben.

"Tiffy," he said, using the nickname she'd never liked. "How are you?"

"Ben. I didn't recognize your number."

"I decided to get a number that matched the area code I live in. And as for what's up, I'm in town."

"Oh. Wow." How was she supposed to respond to that?

"I'd love to get together. Have a coffee and catch up. Any chance you're free?"

"I'm working on a paper, but … just for coffee, right?"

"Yeah. You know, it's been a long time, and, well, I'm trying to catch up with everyone while I'm in town."

Was he catching up with Eric and his parents, too? Because surely Eric would have said something if he knew Ben was in town.

She considered saying no. After all, she really was too busy. But the truth was that she should see him. Maybe she and Eric hadn't discussed it yet, but Ben was the elephant in the room. She needed to make sure Ben knew that she was dating his brother. Not that it was officially his business, but it seemed like the polite thing to do.

"All right. In an hour?"

"Sounds good. I'll swing by and pick you up."

"No, meet me at The Fix. I was about to head there to pick up some papers I left in my cubby." A white lie. There were papers, but she didn't need them. She wanted neutral territory, and her apartment definitely didn't qualify. "We can walk over to Starbucks."

"Perfect. I read about the Man of the Month calendar contest and everything that went on to save the bar. I was hoping to see Tyree and tell him congrats. And see my little brother, before Mom drags him home for a family dinner."

"He's off today," she said. "Same as me."

"No big. He's family, so he'll be around. I'll see you soon."

And that, she thought, *was the problem. Ben was around in Eric and Tiffany's relationship, whether they'd invited him there or not.*

Chapter Five

Not that Eric didn't appreciate Tiffany getting him out of working all day on Tuesday, but once she started to stress about her paper, he'd sent her home. And since he didn't have any other plans, he headed into the bar.

Cam, who was usually off on Tuesdays, was more than happy to cut out and surprise Mina, so Eric slid seamlessly back into his regular routine. Griffin was there, although he'd long ago abandoned his usual place at the bar. Now he was tucked in a corner with Beverly, and Eric had to admit they made a damn cute couple.

Jenna and Reece both used to be regulars at night, but with a two-month-old, Jenna was still officially on leave—though she was working from home—and Reece worked the day shift as much as possible.

Shelby and Nolan sat in a back booth with Amanda and Derek, and they were probably the most boisterous table. Most likely laughing at one of Nolan's off-color joke.

Brent wasn't around, and Eric assumed he was at home with Elena and their daughter, Faith.

And Eric knew that Tyree was in the back with Eva, and would come out periodically to mingle with the regulars and newcomers, just the way a good bar owner should. Tyree, frankly, was Eric's role model, and Eric couldn't have felt prouder that Tyree had offered him the South Congress job if he tried.

All in all, the bar was in fine form tonight. And God knew the customers were keeping Eric on his toes because everyone wanted one of The Fix's specialty drinks. He wasn't the only bartender on duty, but he was the most experienced, and he was doing his best to not only make the drinks quickly, but also put on a bit of a show in the process.

He was popping a lime in a Loaded Corona when the door opened. There was a bell that hung over the door just for show—Faith had bought it at a garage sale for her Uncle Tyree, and he'd immediately hung it over the door—but unless the place was empty, Eric never heard it.

At the moment, though, he was facing that direction and he saw the man walk in. Dark hair. A wrestler's build. And a smile that could cheer up the dourest of rooms.

Ben.

"Eric!" His brother waved to him from the doorway, then hurried over looking like a kid on Christmas morning. "Damn, man, I want to give you a hug but there's two feet of bar between us. Oh well, Mom'll just make us do it later."

"What are you doing here?" Unlike some brothers, Eric and Ben had never had a rough patch. Maybe it was because of the six-year age difference, but they'd always been tight. Which was why it was so damn hard to see him now, with both a bar and a secret between them.

Still, it was also one hell of a nice surprise. "What are you doing in town? I thought you were off being a Yankee."

"Funny man. No, I actually have a job interview at the University."

"I thought you loved your job."

Ben nodded. "I do, but they reached out to me. And can't hurt to talk. And there are lots of good reasons to come back to Austin."

"Like your little brother," Eric said, and Ben smiled.

"Nah. That twerp. I ran as fast as I could."

"Asshole."

"Prick."

"God, I missed you," Eric said. "Want a drink?"

"Can't. I'm not staying. I'm just meeting a date here, then we're heading out."

"Yeah? Who are you meeting?"

But that was a question Eric didn't have to ask. Because she was walking through the door, a smile of greeting on her face and her eyes on Ben. "Ben!" Tiffany said. And then, a split second later, her face went blank. "Eric?"

"Tiffany."

"Hey," Ben said. "I forgot you two work at the same place. Two of my favorite people at the same bar. How sweet is that?"

He slipped his hand around Tiffany's waist, and, Eric noticed, she didn't try to shake it off. Just stood there looking confused.

"I didn't think you were here," she said.

"You two better get going," Eric said. He tossed down a bar rag. "I need to go get some pineapples from the back."

And then he turned and walked away, seething that his brother had returned to take back what was his in the first place, and that Tiffany had intentionally avoided talking about Ben because—as was pretty damn clear now—Eric was just a warm-up for the main act.

Eric slipped away so quickly that Tiffany didn't have time to ask him why he hadn't warned her that Ben was in town. More important, she had no idea if Eric had told his brother that she and Eric were a couple now. She assumed he had—why wouldn't he?—but since she wasn't sure one way or another, she supposed she'd just have to play it by ear. She wondered if Ben had taken it badly. Maybe so, because Eric's mood was definitely off.

She got her usual Grande Flat White and he ordered some drink with a variety of sweeteners and flavors. Eric, she recalled, drank his coffee black. Straight and to the point, she thought. That's how she liked her men.

"You haven't told me why you're in town. Just to see your parents?"

He chuckled. "That's what Eric asked. No, I've got a job interview. At the University."

"Really?" She couldn't decide what she wanted. She knew Eric and Ben were close, but it would be so much less awkward if he were in another state. Still, they weren't dating anymore, and hadn't been for a long time. So how much would he care, anyway? Surely he'd be happy for both of them.

"I'm thinking seriously of taking it if they make me an offer."

She flashed a bright smile. "You miss warm weather."

"I miss you," he said, boldly taking her hand. "I left because of an amazing opportunity, but I never felt like we were finished. I'd like us to keep moving forward. I'd like us to be together. I miss you, Tiffy."

"Oh." She froze for a second, then slowly tugged her hand back. "I—I don't really know how to say this gently. But, well, the truth is..." She drew in a breath. "I'm sorry, Ben. But I don't miss you. Not like that. I—like you a lot. But I don't love you."

"You could."

Her smile was melancholy. "I'm sorry, but I don't think so. Not like you want. As a friend, absolutely." She leaned forward. "And you deserve someone who sees you that way. Who saw you that way in their heart from the very first moment they knew you. She's out there, I'm sure of it. But she isn't me."

"Is there someone else? Someone you love?"

She ran her hands through her hair. "Does it matter? Even if there wasn't, it wouldn't change how I feel—how I *don't* feel—about you."

"And that," he said, "means there is."

She nodded. *Love*. She did. Fast, maybe. But true. "Yeah," she said. "There is. There really is."

Chapter Six

He was being irrational. He knew he was being irrational. And yet Eric still stood in front of her apartment and pounded at the door, waiting for Tiffany to open it, because he damn sure wasn't going away until she did.

"Hey!"

He whipped around and saw her coming up the concrete stairs with a canvas grocery sack.

"What are you doing here?" she asked. "Pleasant surprise, but aren't you supposed to be at The Fix?"

"I called Cam—never mind. We need to talk."

She frowned, then nodded and opened the door, and he was right on her heels. Then he kicked the door closed, turned to face her, and forced himself not to pull her close and kiss her until she renounced all things Ben and promised to only be his.

Instead, he said, "You're still with Ben? You were having a long-distance relationship with my brother and you didn't think to mention it? And then you actually have the nerve to meet him for a date at The Fix—our place. And now you wonder why I'm here? Dammit, Tiffany, why didn't you just ask to borrow a steak knife and jab it in my heart? It would have been kinder."

She stared at him. Just stared, her mouth hanging open a tiny bit. In fact, she stared so long that Eric was beginning to feel as if he were in one of those Sci-Fi movies where the different species wear automatic translation devices. Only hers must be broken, because clearly all she was hearing was garbled words.

"Dammit, Tiffany, say something."

She didn't though. Instead, she burst out laughing.

Which really wasn't the response he'd been expecting. "What the hell?"

"You're an idiot. Adorable, but an idiot."

He cocked his head. "Um. Okay, let's rewind. What?"

"You. Have. It. All. Wrong." She headed toward her kitchen and he followed. "Coffee?"

He only glared.

She smiled sweetly, apparently enjoying herself.

"Tiffany..."

"Your brother and I have not been dating long-distance. On the contrary, I thought his move was a convenient way for me to not have to formally break up with him. I guess I should have, though, because he clearly thought I was still interested. But I wasn't. Don't get me wrong, Ben's a great guy. He's just not my guy."

He nodded, not wanting to interrupt and knock her off track. Because right then, he wanted to hear who *was* her guy.

"When he called me for coffee earlier this evening, I thought that was all it was. Coffee. And I thought that I should probably say something about you and me, although to be honest I was going to play that by ear. I thought maybe you should be the one to tell him. At any rate, I had no date vibes. I had coffee vibes."

She shrugged, then passed him a packet of Oreos. He opened it and ate one, not really paying attention to what he was doing.

"I told him I didn't love him, and he asked me if I was seeing someone. I said I was, but I didn't say it was you." This time her grin was shy. "And then I told him I loved you. Well, the guy I'm seeing. But between you and me, you're the guy."

His head was spinning, but he had definitely focused in on the key word. *Love*.

"Tiffany—I— I'm an idiot."

She snagged an Oreo. "Told you so," she said, then took a bite.

"Love." He swallowed. He loved her, too, but it was too soon to say it. Too soon to do anything about it. "You can't know that," he said. "It's too soon."

She stalked closer, so she was right between his legs. "Don't tell me what I know and don't know."

"But we've only been going out for a couple of days."

"I'm supposed to measure love by a calendar?"

"But—"

"I've known you for years, Eric. You've been in my life—in my heart—for years. I love you. Deal with it." She grinned. "And you know what else? You love me, too." She pressed a finger over his lips. "It's okay if you don't want to say it yet. But just remember who's the psych major. I know what I know."

And he knew she was right, but at the moment, he didn't even care about telling her—after all, he didn't need to. All he wanted was to feel her. To touch her. To claim her so fully and completely that any fear that she belonged to any other man—brother or not—was fully, completely and one hundred percent obliterated.

So he hooked his legs around her, pulled her close, and bent to kiss her. A long, deep kiss. A wild kiss. Her torso was pressed hard between his legs, her body brushing his trapped erection. His tongue dived deep, claiming her. Taking her. It was sex, wild and fast and hot, and he wanted to make her come like this. Wanted to take her to the edge with his mouth on hers and his fingers clutching her hair so that there was no question but that she was his.

"Please," she begged when he broke the kiss, needing air. "Take me to bed."

He released her from his legs, then slid down her body, until his back was to the counter and he was looking at her. *Hell, yes,* his voice screamed in his head. He needed her under him, those sweet noises surrounding him. He needed to bury himself inside her.

But what he said was, "Baby, we can't."

Can't?

Tiffany stared at him. "What do you mean, we can't?"

She watched as Eric dragged a hand through his hair, looking as miserable as she felt. Which was no consolation since she didn't really care about misery loving company. She just wanted him in her bed.

"Eric," she demanded. "What's going on?"

But, of course, she knew the answer even before he said it.

Ben.

"I can't do this—we can't do this—until I've explained everything to my brother."

"What are you talking about? What difference does it make? If he were still in Connecticut we'd be in my bed right now, and I'd be enjoying my fifth orgasm of the evening."

His lips curved up. "Thanks for the compliment."

"Shut up. Explain to me why you're not banging me senseless. And do it in small words and short sentences, because most of my blood is still rushing south." Although she was getting riled up enough now that she'd soon be hyper-coherent.

"Dammit, Tiffany. Don't pretend like you don't understand. He's still in love with you."

"He's in love with the idea of me," she countered, but it didn't matter; he barreled on.

"You know how close we are. Do you really think I can feel good about myself if he's a wreck because of this? If he's not okay with it?"

The words were like a splash of ice water, and she stepped backward until she was opposite him, her back against the kitchen island while his was against the counter. "Wait. Slow down. You're saying this isn't just about telling him what's going on. This is about asking permission? About making sure he's *okay* with it?" She clenched her fists, then unclenched them, trying to regain some control. "In case it escaped your notice, this is not a ménage relationship. Ben doesn't get a vote."

"He's my brother. And he loves you. This will hurt him."

"Him? It's hurting me."

"Tiffany." He took a step toward her, but she twisted away. "So, what if he says he can't deal? Does that mean you just walk away from me?" She was crying now, and she hated that. The taste of salt. The scent of rejection. The confusion that was all churned up inside of her.

"He won't—"

"You don't know that. And what does that say about how you think of me? I'm not his property. He doesn't have the right to claim me and keep me away from you."

"That's not what I'm—"

"Just go."

"Tiffany, please."

But she just shook her head. Too mad and confused and hurt to do anything but push him away. "Please," she said. "Go before I say something I really will regret."

He went, and damn her to hell, she wasn't sure if she was glad he'd obeyed, or pissed off that he hadn't stayed and fought for her.

Chapter Seven

Since Ben was staying at their parents', Eric had called and arranged to have breakfast with them. Which turned out to be one of the most uncomfortable decisions of his life. His parents didn't seem to notice, but there was no way that Ben missed Eric's awkward silence.

He'd never been good at small talk, and sitting through breakfast and not saying what was on his mind to Ben was pure torture.

After, he'd gone out into the backyard. The same yard where he and Ben had played catch for so many years. Where Ben had helped him build a fort. Where they'd played with Muffin, the mutt they'd rescued from the side of the road when Eric was six.

Lots of memories, all good.

Someday, Eric had hoped to get married in this backyard. To say vows under the big oak tree. He still wanted that.

Dammit, he wanted it with Tiffany. Had he really told her it was too soon for her to love him? What kind of an idiot was he? What kind of a person pushed away love?

And what was he doing asking his brother permission to feel?

Shit.

"Hey." Ben leaned against the porch railing, freshly painted as it was every year. And their dad wouldn't let anybody else help or take over the task. "You got something you wanna share with the class?"

"No. Yes. Hell, I don't know."

"Sounds like a yes to me."

Eric sighed. "It's me," he said. "Tiffany's dating me. Or she was. Now she's annoyed with me."

"You?"

Eric lifted a shoulder. "That would be correct."

"Huh." His brother moved to the steps and took a seat. "And now she's pissed? Why?"

"Because I told her I was coming here to make sure you were cool with me and Tiffany going out. But you know what? It doesn't matter if you're cool with it, because I love her. And because she chose me. And I'm really sorry about that, man. I mean truly sorry, but I'm not going to walk away from the best thing to ever happen to me just to keep my brother from having his heart get bruised."

"So you're saying you love her."

"Hell, yeah, I do."

Ben nodded. "And we already know she loves you." He shrugged. "She didn't name names, but I thought the guy was a damn lucky bastard." He met Eric's eyes. "I still do."

"So we're okay?"

"We're golden," Ben said. "I love you both, and I swear I couldn't be happier for you."

"You mean that?" But he could see on Ben's face that he did. "There's someone perfect for you out there, too, you know."

"I know," Ben agreed. "And I'll find her. In the meantime, you should go make up with your girl."

"Explain to Mom and Dad?"

"I'll tell them you had to go see about a girl," Ben said, referencing *Good Will Hunting,* one of their favorite movies.

Eric would have rolled his eyes, but he was already gone.

"I think I screwed up," Tiffany said to Cam and Mina, who she'd called over for an emergency relationship pow-wow. "I know how close he is with Ben, but I got all bent out of shape when he didn't immediately say that it was all about me. About us. He dragged Ben into it, and—"

"Of course you got upset," Mina said. "You don't want anyone else telling Eric who he can and can't love or who he can or can't be with."

"Exactly. But—"

"But at the same time, maybe you should have waited to see what he did before you got all butt hurt?" Cam looked at her and nodded. "I get it, I do. But the guy was in a bad position. He loves you. He loves his brother. His brother loves you."

"So we've established I've handled this all wrong. What do I do now?"

Cam and Mina exchanged glances. "Go find him? Talk to him?"

She frowned. She hated the groveling part. But for Eric, she'd do it.

"I'm gonna go to his place," she said, but when she opened the front door, she saw that Eric had come to her.

"I was just about to knock," he said.

"And we were just about to leave," Mina said, dragging Cam to the door. He caught Tiffany's eyes, a question in his. She nodded, and he kissed her cheek. "For luck," he whispered, then shut the door behind him and Mina.

"I'm sorry," she said to Eric at the same time he said it to her.

"I should never have suggested I needed Ben's permission. I was just…in a weird place."

"Of course you were. Because I put you there. I shouldn't have done that." She bit her lip. "So are we okay?"

"I think we are."

"Thank God. Not being square with you messes with my head."

He grinned. "Mine too."

She drew a breath. "So what happened, anyway?"

"I told him you were mine," he said simply. "That I loved you, and that we're a couple, and he would just have to get used to it."

"Yeah? What did he say?"

"He said he loves us both and he wishes us well. He really does mean it, you know."

She nodded. "I do."

Those two words hung in the air, and their eyes met, a silent *someday* floating between them.

As if to emphasize the point, Eric brushed a soft kiss over her lips. "You're mine, Tiffany. Wholly and completely. Body and soul. And you know what else?"

"What?"

"I'm yours, too."

"I know," she said, her body on fire from his words, his touch. "And now I need you to do something for me."

"What's that?"

"Make love to me."

He grinned, then scooped her up and started toward the bedroom. "Baby, I can do that all night long."

Index

APPETIZERS

DESSERTS

DRINKS

SLICES OF LIFE AND SHORT STORY

Other Books by J. Kenner

The Stark Trilogy:

Release Me

Claim Me

Complete Me

Anchor Me

Lost With Me (coming Oct. 2018)

Stark Ever After:

Take Me

Have Me

Play My Game

Seduce Me

Unwrap Me

Deepest Kiss

Entice Me

Hold Me

Please Me (coming August 2018)

Stark International Steele Trilogy:

Say My Name

On My Knees

Under My Skin

Take My Dare (novella, includes bonus short story: *Steal My Heart*)

Jamie & Ryan Novellas:

Tame Me

Tempt Me

Dallas & Jane (S.I.N. Trilogy):

Dirtiest Secret

Hottest Mess

Sweetest Taboo

Most Wanted:

Wanted

Heated

Ignited

Wicked Nights:

Wicked Grind

Wicked Dirty

Wicked Torture

Man of the Month:

Down On Me

Hold On Tight

Need You Now

Start Me Up

Get It On

In Your Eyes

Turn Me On

Shake It Up

All Night Long

In Too Deep

Light My Fire

Walk The Line

Bar Bites: A Man of the Month Cookbook

Demon Hunting Soccer Mom Series:

Carpe Demon

California Demon

Demons Are Forever

Deja Demon

The Demon You Know

Demon Ex Machina

Pax Demonica

The Dark Pleasures Series:

Caress of Darkness

Find Me in Darkness

Find Me in Pleasure

Find Me in Passion

Caress of Pleasure

Rising Storm:

Tempest Rising

Quiet Storm

The Blood Lily Chronicles:

Tainted

Torn

Turned

The Protector (Superhero) Series:

The Cat's Fancy (prequel)

Aphrodite's Kiss

Aphrodite's Passion

Aphrodite's Secret

Aphrodite's Flame

Aphrodite's Embrace

Aphrodite's Delight (free download)

Other Books by Suzanne McCollum Johnson

Southern Bits & Bites

Southern Kid Bits & Mom Bites

Southern Bits & Bites: Our 150 Favorite Recipes

WRITING WITH LEXI BLAKE

Master Bits & Mercenary Bites

Master Bits & Mercenary Bites~Girls Night

WRITING WITH J. KENNER

Bar Bites: A Man of the Month Cookbook

WRITING WITH LARISSA IONE

Dining with Angels

49577588R10093

Made in the USA
Lexington, KY
24 August 2019